Greener from a Distance
Stories from the Diaspora

Charles Nfon

Langaa Research & Publishing CIG
Mankon, Bamenda

Publisher
Langaa RPCIG
Langaa Research & Publishing Common Initiative Group
P.O. Box 902 Mankon
Bamenda
North West Region
Cameroon
Langaagrp@gmail.com
www.langaa-rpcig.net

Distributed in and outside N. America by African Books Collective
orders@africanbookscollective.com
www.africanbookcollective.com

ISBN: 9956-790-65-6

© Charles Nfon 2013

Table of Contents

Introduction

In transhumance, man and livestock move from the dry pasture in the mountains to the greener grass in the valleys. The reward, the green patches of grass along the banks of rivers and lakes, can often be seen from a distance. So man and animals proceed knowing with some certainty what lies ahead.

Similarly, people move from developing countries to the developed world in search of better lives…seeking greener pastures. However, the greener pasture in that far away country is often a matter of perception. It is a dream, which, in most cases ends up being just that…a dream. Still many around the world yearn to be part of that dream especially the American dream and Albert Ndifon was no exception.

American visit

Albert Ndifon had always wanted to immigrate to the USA but was repeatedly refused a visa. After University, he got a high school teaching job but kept looking for an opportunity to move to the USA. Then he got invited to attend a short course on the role of educators in the promotion of gender equality in Africa.

He booked an appointment for a visa interview at the US embassy in Yaounde. He had become very familiar with the painful process of obtaining a US visa from a third world country. So when he got to the US embassy, he knew how to proceed. He presented his appointment notice and identification to the guard at the embassy gate, who looked at them and asked him to go wait by the narrow gate. He could have let Albert in immediately but he had to display the significance of being a guard at the US embassy.

The guard, a tall middle age man of Cameroonian nationality, had an air of superiority about him. He felt like a mini god holding the keys to paradise and displayed a total lack of respect for local visa seekers. When an American or any white person showed up, he flipped from master to servant, rushing to open the gate and seeking notice by waving frantically.

Ten minutes later, he let Albert in. Despite having a 10 AM appointment, Albert had to wait in line. It was a first come first serve affair. Just like with the doctors, an appointment guaranteed that you would be seen on a given day, not necessarily at a given time.

The line was long, given the presence of many other American dream chasers. Standing in line was not an issue because everyone ended up having his chance with a visa officer that same day. Other embassies were worse when it came to the visa procedure.

Albert's friend had spent a night outside the British High Commission, hoping to make it inside for a visa audience. He was one of many that night and some had paid professional "linesmen" to hold spots for them overnight. Many usually braved the rain, heat, humidity, mosquitoes, sexual predators and other dangers just to reserve a place on the queue. Then the gate opened and they let people in one by one. When the cut off for the day was attained, the rest were sent home, whether they had spent the night at the gate or not. After all that trouble, most were usually denied visas.

There were lots of entertaining stories from these American dream chasers which made waiting in line kind of fun. People took the liberty of revealing how their invitation letters, other documents and bank statements were obtained. Interestingly, the most vocal ones usually had fake documents; the kind of documents produced and doctored in Bonamousadi by local experts for a handsome fee.

Possible questions and prepared answers were discussed. Others disclosed their intentions of not returning to Cameroon after attending the short conference or seminar they were invited to. There were also those invited for a relative's graduation or marriage ceremony with the ultimate plan being to remain in the US after the occasion. All these people made no secret of their plans, which was foolish. Knowing the Americans, spies could easily have been planted in the line to weed out the fake applicants.

The loudest dream chaser of the day was a young man called Nick. He had nicknamed himself *man-for-doky*, as a testament to his ability to manufacture fake documents. Nick was the kind of guy who enjoyed the spot light. He proudly displayed his fake invitation letter, fake bank statement, a fabricated letter of support from a prominent minister and a fake marriage certificate. He compared his documents with anyone who cared to do so, daring them to spot anything that would betray his fakes. He even carried counterfeit money on him and claimed he would spend it in the embassy. Reaction to Nick was mixed, ranging from disgust to indifference to admiration.

Interestingly, those with genuine documents and clean motives were usually the very modest and quiet ones in the crowd. A family of four stood a short distance behind Nick. Vincent, Rose and their two children had not shown any interest in Nick or his antics. He hated being ignored, so he moved over to talk to them. It was easy to tell he was Anglophone because he struggled with the French language. He was the type who would try to impress people by speaking French, only to succeed in torturing those who understood the language!

"*Bonjour monsieur. C'est ton deux enfants ça? C'est ton famille?* " Nick started, in bad French.

"*Oui, c'est ma famille*" Vincent replied. "*Ce sont mes deux enfants*" he continued. "Can we just speak English? You know English is the official language in the USA right."

"Yes I know that. I know everything about the USA. I learn a lot by watching movies and talking to my friends" Nick said. "You must have spent a lot of money to get all the documents for the whole family. What is your story?" he continued.

"My story? What do you mean?" Vincent replied, feeling disgust but staying calm. "By the way I did not spend any money to get documents. I merely requested for them from my employer" he continued.

"Employer? Where do you work? You mean you did not grease the big man's elbows for his recommendation letter or something like that?" Nick inquired.

"I work in the US. With very few exceptions, people don't generally accept bribes out there. You make a request, they study it and they grant it if it is within the law" Vincent shared.

"Whoa, you are a bushfaller! *So you be American wander!* Can I see your passport sir? Can I see how the visa looks like?" Nick asked wide eyed with excitement.

Vincent immediately regretted sharing that much information. This guy could be a thief for all he knew. If he was such a cheat, what would have stopped him from being an armed robber? Coming from America was usually sufficient to make one a target for thieves. If Nick was part of a gang, he could easily track them back to their residence and plan a late night attack. He had to avoid giving away any further information.

But Nick pressed him for more. "Why are you here, on this line, with us if you work in America? You are lying to me right?" Nick queried.

"My wife and kids need visas to join me in the USA, okay. Can you leave me alone now please?" Vincent said, desperate to get rid of Nick.

"Okay Mr. America. By the way, I will see you there if you make it back" retorted an angry Nick as he made his way back to his spot. The subtle threat did not go unnoticed.

At the end of the day, those who received permission to visit the USA jubilated as they stepped out of the embassy, making sure everyone else noticed. A silent exit in most cases usually meant the visa request had been declined.

Sadly, many with fake documents or unscrupulous plans were granted visas while some good intentioned applicants never got the nod. Reasons for rejection ranged from lack of family ties in Cameroon to lack of investments or property, implying the applicants would not return home if they got to the USA.

This time, Albert had covered all his bases. He had come clean on previous occasions and had failed. He still had clean documents for the most part except for the inflated bank statement and fake land title. And this time, he got the visa. Yes, Albert was allowed to visit the USA. His visa was valid for six months, long enough for a lot to happen in the USA after his short course, provided he even went for the course.

Nick was unsuccessful at obtaining a visa. His fraudulent ways had not fooled the Americans. However, he was not turned over to the local police for fraud. There was no point. For a small bribe, he would have been freed almost immediately.

2

America here I come

Albert chose to depart from Douala airport. Though his flight was late Tuesday night, he chose to leave Yaounde for Douala a day earlier. It turned out to be a wise decision because the head of state, aka Lionman, was visiting Douala on Tuesday. The main roads in Yaounde were blocked to all commercial traffic early Monday evening. Elements of the presidential guard lined the streets from the presidency to the airport. Tall buildings along the way had guards on roof tops and balconies. Businesses were paralyzed late Monday and early Tuesday until after the Lionman's departure. The airports in Douala and Yaounde were almost at a standstill on Tuesday morning. In Douala, elements of the presidential guard were also stationed along the streets from the airport to Lionman's destination. The main highway from Yaounde to Douala was closed 50 km from each city.

The situation in the two cities had the semblance of a state of emergency. To mask this, the ruling party rallied its militants, dressed them in colorful uniforms and put them at strategic locations. Jobless and hungry citizens were also lured in with the promise of beer and food.

Inhabitants of Yaounde were accustomed to these charades because Lionman left his den at least once every two months to spend three months in either Switzerland or France. His departure and return to the den always engineered this quasi state of emergency and the associated loss of revenue from paralysis of businesses and services including hospitals, restaurants, bars, taxis, roadside vendors and office workers who could not make it to work.

Had Albert chosen to leave Yaounde on Tuesday, it would have been difficult to get to the bus station on the other side of the city. At best, he would have departed late afternoon.

Albert left for the airport once normalcy returned to Douala. He got there in time for check in. The check in line was long and slow. Passengers with excess luggage made it even slower as they argued about the extra levy.

A restless man in front of Albert looked familiar. The man kept looking at his passport, passing his fingers over the photo and looking nervously at police officers who passed by. He seemed even more nervous when his turn came to check in. There was a brief conversation between him and the clerk. The clerk left and returned with a police officer in tow who immediately took the man's passport. The ensuing conversation was loud enough for everyone to hear.

"Is this your passport?" the officer asked.

"What kind of question is that?" retorted the man. "Don't you see my photo in there?" he continued.

Albert immediately recognized that voice and the face. That was Nick, the cheat; the man who had been so vocal at the US embassy. He had been without the goatee and glasses the last time Albert had seen him. This was probably an attempted disguise.

"Don't talk to me like that" the officer warned Nick. "You don't want me to invite my men right now, do you?"

"That is my passport sir. Please, can we talk in your office?" Nick said, trying to avoid the public spectacle.

"We are going to talk right here. Tell me the truth, is this your passport?" the officer asked again. By this time other police officers had accompanied their boss and were ready for some action, Cameroonian style.

"It is a long story sir. Let's go to your office and I will tell you everything. I also have some money that I don't need to take to the USA" Nick continued to plead.

"Are you trying to bribe me? I am a respectable superintendent of police. I can add attempted bribery and corruption to your list of crimes. By the way, you have not told me if this is your passport or not."

Albert wondered what the police boss meant by respectable. The fact that he sends others to collect bribes on his behalf doesn't free him of any guilt. Respectable when there is an audience of locals and foreigners but cash grabbing jerk when there are no spectators.

"Officer, you see, I am also a respectable citizen going to seek a better life abroad. I have not harmed anybody, you know" Nick continued to ramble.

Did Nick refer to himself as a respectable citizen? He definitely used 'respectable' in the same context as the police officer……. respectable thief and cheat.

"*Qui s'excuse s'accuse.* You know what I mean! You are exhibiting all the signs of a criminal. May I see your national identity card" the officer asked.

"But I don't need a national identity card to leave the country. I left it at home."

The officer ran out of patience, turned to the junior officers around him and ordered them into action.

"Arrest this criminal immediately" he said. "Bring all his belongings to my office for a thorough search."

Nick feeling cornered, made a mad dash for the nearest exit. The sound of a whistle alerted other police officers to the fleeing Nick. He was subdued, kicked and punched before being taken to detention. Despite more beating and kicking, Nick refused to answer the important questions.

The police boss urged his men to up the torture a notch and a broken nose broke Nick's resolve. A confession was extracted from him.

Shortly afterwards a junior police officer repeated Nick's confession and parts of a report they had on file from the victims of a crime which matched Nick's story. Albert was part of a small audience that had formed around this proud junior officer.

Nick was the head of a notorious gang in Yaounde. After failing to obtain a visa from the US embassy, Nick and his gang had tracked a man in possession of one. The man had been suspicious and had taken extra precautions that night. He lived in a house surrounded by a high fence with barb wire at the top, prisoner in his own property like most rich people in Cameroon. That night he bought an iron chain and a stronger lock for the gate, blocking the main entrance into the house with furniture and having everyone ready to dial the police on their cell phones should anything strange happen.

The gang arrived and tried to get into the man's compound without success but decided to hang around in case someone came home late. The man's junior brother had gone out that night without informing anyone. On returning, he was immediately surrounded at the gate by the gang and instructed on what to do. The elder brother was summoned to the gate by his junior sibling. He failed to notice the thieves hiding in the shadows with their guns pointing at both brothers. It wasn't until they entered the living room that the elder brother noticed the gang. One thief stayed with each of the brothers while the rest ransacked the building. The rest of the family was locked up in the washroom and instructed not to move. This day, they regretted having a washroom with an external lock.

Nick requested for the elder brother's passport, money and cell phones.

After collecting all they could, Nick wanted one more thrill; to kick and punch the elder of the brothers. When this torturing commenced, the junior brother could not resist the urge to fight. He sprang up and punched Nick in the face leaving him with a bloodied nose. This infuriated Nick and he immediately discharged his weapon into his attacker's chest, killing him instantly. Another thief shot the elder brother in the arm and assumed him dead as the gang hurried out of the compound.

One child had taken a cell phone into the washroom and they had called the police as the drama was unfolding in the living room. According to the police report, they arrived one hour later, after the gang had already left.

Typical of the Cameroonian police, Albert said to himself. *They always wait enough time to avoid a run in with the gang. It is a postmortem kind of police not an intervention force. None of them wants to die rescuing a citizen from the hands of thieves. To them, heroism is measured by how much money is brought back from a traffic patrol, not by service to or sacrifices for mankind.* Albert was so consumed in his thoughts that he missed a chunk of the story.

The washroom prisoners were eventually freed. The elder brother was taken to the hospital where he recovered successfully though with a paralyzed arm.

The thieves were not caught, the police claiming to be still searching for the gang.

Nick had glued his passport photo into the stolen passport, concealing that of the original owner. It would have been hard to detect had the police and airline staff not been on the lookout for this.

Nick named the rest of his gang under further torture. Some of them had been at the airport and had left immediately but were arrested on a bus to Yaounde. The others were arrested in Yaounde.

"You know what? The owner of that passport works in America. He promised a huge reward in dollars for anyone who recovered his passport. My boss is going to receive this money and we will get nothing, not even five francs. Selfish pig, that guy" the junior officer whispered to Albert who had taken a vantage position in his audience.

"Who is the owner of the passport?" Albert asked.

"Look at him!" the officer said frustrated with Albert's question. "I am complaining about big dollars and all you care about is the owner of the passport. If you must know, his name is Vincent Nonen."

Albert immediately connected the dots. Vincent was the family man who had humiliated Nick at the US embassy and had received a subtle threat.

What a way to depart my beloved country, Albert thought, as he boarded the plane. Standing close to a dangerous robber, witnessing a police interrogation and an arrest with what the Americans might call the use of excessive force. To a thief, excessive police force was a lesser evil than mob justice.

After learning Nick's crime, the crowd had wanted him released to them for severe beating. Some had readied gasoline to pour on him and burn him alive. It would have been gruesome and Albert was grateful it did not happen. He would have arrived the land of dreams with nightmares; Nick the talkative cheat and robber roasting away, probably still rambling in English and broken French; that would have been unforgettable.

The police arrest could be considered a happy ending; a bad guy and his crew taken off the streets. Yes that sounded American; *Americans love happy endings*, Albert concluded as he settled down in his seat on the plane.

America, here comes Albert Ndifon at long last, and good bye to Lionman's personal jungle, he said to himself.

3

At the airport

Albert flew into the Hartford International Airport. Fatigued from the flight, he wanted to get to his friend's house as soon as possible. However, immigration and customs agents awaited.

His flight was one of many that arrived at the same time. Travelers were separated into two groups; the Americans on one side and the rest of the world on the other side. The Americans went through immigration and customs at a faster pace, occasionally glancing over at the rest of the world, some with a smile, others with indifference, some with a smirk and others with disgust. Was this a sign of what to expect in America; some sort of segregation, acceptance, tolerance and outright hatred or rejection?

Finally it was Albert's turn to be cleared by an immigration agent.

"Welcome to America. May I have your passport please" the agent said.

Albert gave him his passport and other relevant documents. The agent flipped through the passport, looked up at Albert, repeated the process 4-5 times, asked Albert to go sit in a waiting area and left for the back office.

At this point, stories of people sent back to Cameroon from their point of entry began flashing through Albert's mind. One of these was a man who had traveled with his elder brother's passport. The brothers had a strong resemblance and the younger brother had easily fooled the officers in Cameroon. Either that or he had sacrificed a large sum of money in exchange for a blind eye.

For some reason, the brothers did not have the same last name. When the younger brother got to the airport in America, his travel documents were thoroughly checked. He was asked to wait as the agent went to the back office. A few minutes later, the agent came back to the waiting area and called out for Mr. en di en wa (Ndinwa) to come with him to the office. No one moved. He repeated the name, this time saying the first name (Julius) and the country of origin. Again, no one moved. The officer decided to match the face on the passport to the faces in the waiting area and quickly spotted the brother.

"What is your name sir?" the agent asked.

"Meyme Kilian" the younger brother replied giving his real name. All the coaching he had received had evaporated.

Puzzled, the agent asked him his date of birth and he gave a different date from that in the passport. The agent showed him the passport and asked if he recognized it. The younger brother realized his mistake. He was taken to the back office and his story quickly unraveled. He attempted to explain why his previous answers were wrong and that the passport belonged to him. He tried to blame it on the agent's poor pronunciation of the name. In his native land, the letter "n" in Ndinwa was not emphasized the way the agent did. He also tried to blame his confusion on jetlag and fatigue but this got him nowhere. He was detained and deported on the next available flight to Cameroon.

The second story was about a guy who had obtained a counterfeit visa. He spent one million francs for this visa; money his parents borrowed from friends and relatives with the promise to pay back once their son got to America and started earning big dollars. His flight was also paid for with money from sold land and his parents' savings. A lavish going away party was organized on the eve of his departure, with many young women in attendance hoping to hook up with the America bound guy, their own potential passage to the land of dreams.

On the day of departure, he negotiated his way through the local customs and immigration officers with more of his family's hard earned cash.

When he got to his port of entry in the USA, his visa was quickly detected as fake. When asked where he obtained his visa he arrogantly replied "from your embassy, of course."

More questions followed and he could feel his American dream slipping away. He felt it was time to follow the advice from his friends. He had been told to be bold and assert his rights if he faced tough questions. That is what people do in America, they had told him. So he started to yell at the immigration agent.

"This is a genuine visa. Do you think I am a crook? Do you know who you are talking to? I will sue if you continue to delay me here. My brother is waiting for me over there. He is a powerful man and he can cause you so much trouble if you don't let me go now."

In his country, this kind of talk might have induced some fear and gotten the desired results. There, powerful people can do hurtful things to the weak and helpless. So people tend to cave in when threatened with empty talk. But in America, empty talk takes you nowhere and power has its limits most of the time.

Instead, the yelling caused the agent to stand his ground and get reinforcement. The guy was detained and put on the next flight back to Cameroon. He returned broke and ashamed and could hardly lift his head up. If he had a tail it would have perpetually remained between his legs. Indeed, his reflection of a tail stayed without action for a long time. The women who had failed to get his attention at his going away party enjoyed his misery. Even the chosen one also left him, in search of the next and hopefully genuine America bound.

Stories of deportations were still flashing through Albert's mind when, finally, the immigration agent returned and called his name, or rather what sounded like his name.

"Mr en-di-fon Albert!" It sounded like a question. Albert hesitated for a moment. The agent called out his name again. "Can Mr en-di-fon Albert from Cameroon come forward, please?" Albert recognized his name in "*American*".

What is wrong with these people, he thought. *I just heard them say Nicolas without pounding the "N" but for some reason they have to stress the "N" in African names.*

Albert answered a series of questions. The agent looked satisfied, completed the rest of the formalities and sent Albert on his way.

After baggage claim, came the customs. Albert had brought some native food for his friends. A search of his luggage yielded dried cowpea leaves, a delicacy from his part of Cameroon. Unfortunately, the dried leaves resembled pot. This called for special attention and additional custom officers. This also meant another lengthy delay while the package was verified. Finally, a man emerged and declared the dried leaves as some herbs of no known nutritional or medicinal value. That was an insult to Albert but he did not mind taking one as long as they let him step foot on American soil outside the confines of the airport. After scaling this last hurdle, he moved to the waiting area where his friend was scheduled to meet him.

Albert's friend, Samson, was delayed at work and then in the heavy traffic to the airport. Albert could wait anyway, he concluded. After having waited so long to get to America, what would a few hours in an American airport cost him?

The airports in America are clean, have good entertainment options and Albert would not be bored waiting, Samson assumed.

Samson smiled as he recalled his father arriving at the airport during his first visit to the USA. He had gone to the washroom, had come out and had declared that the washroom was so clean one could comfortably have lunch in there without worrying about germs. He had marveled at the sweet scents in the toilet. Samson had told him the cleanliness did not completely preclude the presence of germs. About the scents, Samson had said to him to be weary of what they concealed; usually a generous spray of air freshener meant the worst stinker had just been released by the previous visitor. Samson's father had said he would take invisible germs and concealed odors over maneuvering on tip toes in a pool of urine and being welcomed by toilets filled with other people's waste.

Remembering the glass door incident, Samson smiled and shook his head at the same time. The first three doors his father had gone through at the airport were automatic sliding doors. Each time he had prepared to open the door and was amazed as it parted by itself. He had gotten used to the luxury of VIP treatment from doors. Then he came to one that required pushing a button to activate the not so automatic opening. He walked straight into the glass door, head first. He had sworn in his native language, and then said his mother's name over and over again. At 60, he was still a mama's boy. A bump had developed on his forehead and was dubbed his welcome to America official stamp. Samson had said "dad that is your right to stay in America, right there in the open for everyone to see."

Samson was not smiling when it came to the highway patrol incident. He and his dad were visiting some friends down south. Samson went above the speed limit and was stopped by the highway patrol officers. Before they could blink, the officers had their guns drawn and pointed at both of them. They were ordered out of the vehicle and made to lie down on their stomachs. After searching them and the vehicle and finding no weapons or drugs, they were allowed back in and given a speeding ticket on top of that. His dad had been really shaken and decided to return to Cameroon even sooner.

Albert was relieved when Samson arrived, they talked briefly and Samson apologized profusely as he explained his lateness. Determined to escape the airport parking fees, they quickly loaded Albert's luggage into the vehicle and left. Rush hour was over, making the drive to Samson's home seem short.

Samson took the next day off to show his friend around.

4

Identity Relay

On the weekend, Albert and Samson attended a birthday party for a five year old kid. It was hard to tell the age of the kid from the amount of planning and the guest list. There were more adults than kids; and the kids were relegated to the background when the party started. Just like Christmas nowadays.

After eating and drinking came the dancing. Albert was amazed at a man in the mid-sixties trying to outdo everybody on the dance floor.

"Who is that old man?" Albert asked Samson. "Look at him; he has some spectacular Makossa moves."

"That is Pa Mola. Old man Mola's story is complicated. Let me see if I can summarize it for you" Samson replied.

Pa Mola came to the USA decades ago. He stayed in the country illegally and did not go back to Cameroon for several years. Eventually he "*regularized*" his stay in the US. Then he started visiting Cameroon at least once every year.

People still laugh when he tells how he met Ellen, his American wife. Ellen was a cashier at a grocery store. Mola went to the store for groceries a week after he arrived the US. Ellen was friendly, always smiling and chatting with customers; just doing her job the way she was trained. Mola had not noticed that she treated every customer the same. When she smiled and chatted with him at check out, Mola gave it a greater significance than it was worth. Just like Charles in Nyamnjoh's *The Disillusioned African* who was tempted to give more meaning than it was due to his landlady's *my love*.

Mola hurried home to tell his friend that the lady at the store was into him; he might just have found himself a girlfriend already, he said. His friend had laughed, telling him it was just good customer service and nothing more.

Mola had just come from a country where good customer service in big stores was almost nonexistent. Any descent customer service in his country was reserved for white tourists and influential people. Rudeness was common and a smile was rare when dealing with the average person. Complaints and grievances from customers were usually settled with insults, ejection from the store and sometimes physical fights. That was in stark contrast to what Mola had just experienced.

To convince himself, he dragged his friend back to the store and went straight to check out without any groceries.

"How can I help you, sir?" Ellen asked with the usual smile.

"You don't remember me? I was here not long ago?" Mola asked, with a shy smile and a slightly confused look.

"No I don't remember you. Did you forget something?" Ellen asked, with genuine concern.

"No. You were so nice to me. You smiled at me. I came back to see you" Mola said.

Ellen stopped smiling and put on the most serious face she could muster.

"Thank you for the compliment sir. I am just doing my job. All our customers are special to us, so we serve them with a smile. Now, if you will excuse me, I have other valuable customers to attend to."

"Can you believe that guy? That was so weird and creepy" Ellen said to the next customer who had been waiting patiently.

Mola's friend laughed at him and gave him some serious advice.

"That kind of behavior can get you into trouble my friend. You are in a different society now; you have to be very careful. Just looking at a woman the wrong way can earn you a sexual harassment charge, not to talk of touching her. No unsolicited phone calls, no visits without an invitation and never assume anything unless there is an explicit consent. Most importantly, don't show any sexual interest in a minor, it is just wrong and will ruin the rest of your life.

"Also, never stop to give a female stranger a ride. That is solicitation or an attempted kidnapping. I am telling you these things because I know in your country sexual harassment is rampant. The boss tries to sleep with every female in his office and torments those who turn him down; dirty talk and sexually explicit acts directed at women are common and even encouraged. And people stop for any beautiful woman at the roadside. If you have any of that left in you, please wash it off now before it lands you in jail." Mola felt insulted but deep inside he appreciated the advice.

"Always remember, to borrow from Nyamnjoh's wisdom, the cashiers in this country smile at your money not at you. Like robots, they are programmed to be nice to anybody who has money to spend" Mola's friend continued.

Three months later Mola got a job at the same store. Ellen remembered him and nicknamed him weirdo. Coming from a different culture with differences in the use of words, as portrayed in the following conversation, helped bolster Mola's reputation as a weirdo.

"My neighbor has a pussy. That monster stares at me through the window each time I pass by" Mola told Ellen.

"What are you talking about? Are you a peeping tom, or is she sick, exposing herself to you that way?" Ellen asked surprised.

"My neighbor is a man. No he is not sick" Mola replied.

"What, a man with emmm emmm, whatever, a pussy? Am I missing something or what?" Ellen asked.

"Oh, now I see what you are thinking. I am talking about a pussy cat. Where I come from we call them pussies" Mola explained.

"I see. We prefer to call them cats. The p word is used for a woman's private part" Ellen told him.

"Thanks. I will never forget this" Mola said, laughing, as he walked away from an embarrassed Ellen.

On another occasion Mola and Ellen were talking about the difficulty of getting up early for the morning shift.

"When my alarm goes off, I push the snooze button and go back to sleep" Ellen said.

"It is easier to use a cock. It will disturb you until you get out of bed. Those things can be persistent, you know" Mola said.

"That is very inappropriate Mister. You better watch your words. I am okay without a cock" Ellen said, beginning to turn red.

"What did I say wrong again? It is true, in most villages in my country cocks, not alarm clocks, wake people up early in the morning. The big cocks usually do the best job" Mola continued, apologetic in his tone.

'OK. I am missing something again. What are you talking about?" Ellen asked.

"Cock, the opposite of hen? The bird that crows, that is what I am talking about" Mola explained.

"Oh my, I got it all wrong again. That your word stands for a male private part. We prefer rooster" Ellen said.

"Thank you again." Then he put his finger to his lips and looked intensely at Ellen. "It is funny how sensitive you are to these words" he continued, "but you swear fuck over small inconveniences. When I hear that I imagine a monster cat swallowing a rooster."

On another occasion, Mola overheard Ellen talking to another colleague.

"I like your pants. Where did you get them from?" Ellen asked.

"A friend gave them to me. They are nice, aren't they? They fit very nicely" the colleague replied.

After the colleague left, Mola wanted to understand what they were talking about.

"You can see her pants? What kind of eyes do you have, x-ray?" Mola asked.

"What are you talking about?" Ellen looked perplexed. "Everybody can see her pants. You saw her pants, didn't you?"

Mola laughed. "I wish, but I did not see them. I only saw her trousers."

"Oh my, you are thinking about her underpants, aren't you? You rotten guy" Ellen said, rather disgustedly.

"In my country pants are worn under trousers or skirts, or whatever. The outer long things are called trousers" Mola explained.

"Pants or underpants, I hope you never see them, weirdo!" Ellen retorted.

Over time, Ellen gradually warmed up to Mola. Despite, or perhaps because of, his strange way with words, she considered him funny. They became friends and started spending time together after work.

Mola wanted so much to take it to the next level but his friend's advice kept ringing in his ears. *Don't assume anything and don't move too fast*, he told himself.

Eventually, he asked her out on a date. She had been expecting it and readily said yes. They went to a modest restaurant bar. Mola avoided any discussion about his life before America. They went out on many more dates before Mola considered getting very intimate.

When the time came, it started awkwardly. Ellen initiated a kissing session which was clearly an upward indication of a mid-body desire. Melting under his arms, she failed to notice his eyes searching around for something. He pulled away suddenly, startling Ellen in the process.

"What is the matter? You don't want me?" she asked. "I thought you wanted this as much as I did."

"Oh yeah, I want it so much. I am sorry. My friend told me there has to be an explicit consent before going to second base. I was wondering if it should be written. What do you think?" he asked.

"Don't be silly. I just told you how much I want it. Come over here, you. This cat is more than ready to consume that enormous rooster. Don't leave me hanging!" Ellen urged him, accompanied by seductive hip, head and eye movements. Mola pounced like a hungry lion. Ten minutes later his roar of satisfaction was load. It was mutual satisfaction, though Ellen's exclamations were muted in the background.

They continued to see each other until Mola went to another city for training. When they met again three years later, they got married.

They had their only child two years into their marriage. Jessica was a beautiful little girl, a bundle of joy. Mola and Ellen adored her. She had her mother's blue eyes and her father's broad nose and an infectious smile characteristic of both parents. She was a daddy's girl for the first five years. He bragged about her to anybody who cared to listen but it was mom who bought her all the trendy toys and Barbie dolls. Mola did not believe in having a drawer full of toys for one kid.

Mola's parents never bought him any toys, not because they did not love him, but because they could not afford them. He made his own toys. His favorite toy was a small car he made using old plank and rusted nails recovered from old furniture. The wheels were made out of old slippers that he painstaking carved using his father's old shaving blade. He occasionally cut himself and knew exactly what kind of leaves to moisten and squeeze into the wound for treatment.

Mola also complained when Ellen bought multiple beach balls for Jessica.

"This is a waste of money. How many beach balls can a little girl play with?" Mola protested.

"But they are different colors. She can switch between colors. I should even buy a different color for each day of the week" Ellen replied.

"Kids in this country are all spoiled. As a kid I had to make my own soccer ball out of old cloth and rubber. I would wrap the cloth into a ball and then use the rubber strings to keep it in shape" Mola started.

"Yes I know! I have heard that story many times already. You and your friends played the ball on dirt roads, you all had no shoes because your parents could not afford them, and you remember the time you hit your toe on a rock and lost the nail" Ellen interjected.

"Exactly, I am glad you remember. Little Jessica already has a closet full of shoes that she will soon outgrow and you keep buying her more shoes. Not to talk about Christmas presents. Does a child need a room full of presents? Presents that she will open, throw aside and never touch again for the rest of the year. That is wastage. Anyway I will take some of them with me when next I go to Cameroon" Mola rambled.

"Of course, your poor sponsored kids in Cameroon will appreciate that. You see, nothing is going to waste and we are making you look generous" Ellen concluded.

By age six, Jessica's personality was beginning to show. She had a strong will and almost always had a response to everything. She argued and talked back to her parents. When Jessica began showing these signs of stubbornness, Mola considered corporal punishment.

The problem was, this kind of punishment was not allowed in America. Besides, Ellen was not on board with that kind of discipline. But Mola grew up in a system where you listened and did what you were told, or received a serious beating. Mola remembered his father having a cane besides his favorite chair in the living room. Each time he called a kid in a particular tone, it meant there was some explaining to do, and if he was not satisfied with the explanation, he easily reached over for his cane. Do not spare the rod because it will spoil the child, was his motto as well as that of many other parents. It was even an acceptable form of discipline in schools.

"She is getting out of control. We need to handle her with a firm hand, else she will end up with her pants on the ground and her navel perpetually exposed like many of those girls out there. A little bit of whipping will tell her when to shut up and listen" Mola told his wife.

"No, you are not hitting my daughter. If you dare, I will throw you out of this house and report you to child welfare. The kid is just expressing herself. What you see as a negative today might be her greatest assert in the future. Let's try positive reinforcement and alternative ways of discipline" Ellen emphasized.

"This so called assert can only lead to trouble for you and me in the future. If we are not careful, her strong headedness will cause one of us a heart attack someday. I rest my case" Mola surrendered, reluctantly.

Pa Mola continued to visit Cameroon on a regular basis, but never took his family with him. Jessica always wanted to go, but her father used scare tactics to dissuade her. He told her his part of the country was very dangerous, they would be kidnapped and possibly killed if a ransom was not paid; that some people were still killed after the ransom was paid.

Jessica had the chance to talk to a young boy who had just returned from Cameroon.

"Did you see any kidnappers in Cameroon?" Jessica asked.

"What are kidnappers anyway?" the boy had asked

"These are bad people who take away foreign kids, hide them in a dark place and ask for money from the kids' parents. If no money is given, the kids are killed" Jessica repeated what her father had told her.

"No way, there is nothing like that in that country. Little kids play by themselves all over the place and nothing happens to them. It is not like here where mom and dad have to watch you while you play in the park. Kids just run around by themselves, go to the stream or the public tap to fetch water by themselves and even go to the soccer field on the other side of town by themselves, and always return home" the boy told Jessica.

"But those are local kids. My dad says the bad guys target only American kids" Jessica explained.

"I played outside by myself and nothing happened to me. They had chickens and goats roaming the yard. I would go outside and run after the chickens and scare them. I loved the noise they made when I scared them. The goats were more bold, especially the baby goats; they are also called kids, you know. They were so cute. They would run towards me, stop, jump and spin around and then bounce away as if daring me to catch them. I loved watching them play around" the boy said.

"Now I really want to go there and see these things for myself. How about the food, did you like it?" Jessica asked.

"Not all of it but my mom carried lots of snacks which I ate whenever I did not like the food. It was the harvest season, so there was a lot of fresh food. I liked eating roasted corn, boiled fresh peanuts, bananas, roasted plantains and roasted fish. There was a large variety of food, including fruits, making it difficult to go hungry" the boy went on.

"When I am old enough to travel by myself, I will go there. I will not tell my parents or I will tell them that I am going somewhere else" Jessica confessed.

"What, you are going to lie to your parents? That is bad. You will be grounded, if not spanked or both" the boy said.

"Well, my dad leaves me no choice. At that age I will be using my own money, so no one will be grounding me anymore. By the way, do your parents spank you?" Jessica asked.

"No, no way" the boy replied and ran off to join his mother. Jessica could tell he was lying.

Although Mola's stories about kidnappers were not corroborated by any other person, his family chose to trust and believe him.

However, when his strong willed daughter turned 16 she began asking more questions and pushing him for details about these dangers that seemed unique to his family and not the others who went to Cameroon all the time.

"Dad, I think you are just keeping us away from your family in Cameroon. Are you ashamed of something?" Jessica asked.

"Stop talking like that. There is no reason for you to go there. It is expensive for all of us to go. When they kidnap you who will pay the ransom? I don't want to put you in danger" her father replied.

"But other kids from the same part of Cameroon go once in a while. Only your kid seems to be in danger. Why?" she asked.

"Stop asking me all these questions. Your mother is not interested in going to that country. What is the matter with you? This is the last time we are discussing this, understand!" her father said, rather angrily, and stormed out of the room.

His outburst only enforced her suspicion that he was hiding something from them. She was determined to find out. She had to do it alone. Her mother was truly not interested in going there. The one time she had shown an interest in travelling to Cameroon, her cousin had discouraged her.

"You want to go there, Ellen? With all the mosquitoes, snakes, cholera, poverty and desperation, and all what your husband has told you about kidnappers? You must be out of your mind" her cousin had said, making Mola's day.

At 18, Jessica decided to visit Cameroon but told her family that she was vacationing in Mexico. She had gotten information about hotels, bus travel and directions to her father's hometown from his close friend, Bruno.

"Jessica, I am giving you this information in confidence" Bruno said. "Your father is my best friend. This is betrayal and if he knows about this he will never talk to me."

"Trust me, Bruno. I will not tell anybody. I will act like a professional journalist; never reveal my sources. I am also counting on you to keep my travel plan a secret" Jessica told Bruno. "Can you at least give me a hint on what to expect when I get to his home? Anything?" she asked.

"I have given you enough information. I have already betrayed my friend enough. I will let you go discover the rest for yourself. There will be no need to go if you already know what to expect. I admire your courage for embarking on this journey. It is a journey in many ways" Bruno said. "Have a safe journey."

"Thank you."

Jessica was convinced Bruno knew something disturbing about her father but was reluctant to tell.

Jessica's trip took her through France, Equatorial Guinea and then Douala, Cameroon. The flight from America to France was great. Everything was orderly, the flight attendants were friendly and respectful and the service was almost impeccable.

The same could not be said about the flight to Douala. Getting on the plane was chaotic, with almost every passenger carrying oversized hand luggage. The flight attendants were the complete opposite of the ones on the previous flight operated by the same airline. They were loud, rude and disrespectful. It seemed a mean switch was suddenly turned on when it came to flights on this route. Were the attendants trained for this or was it a customer driven behavior? It was service probably reserved for a certain class of customers.

The flight attendants really had a good handle on this meanness switch, turning it off seamlessly when the right customer had an on flight request. However, it was hard to blame them for this adaptation. Newton's law of motion states that for every action there is an equal and opposite reaction. These flight attendants might have modified this law for their job on this route; for every chaotic customer there is a tough and decisive customer service.

There was calm once the plane took off, except for the occasional loud passengers who engaged in animated conversations and raucous laughter with no regard for their sleeping neighbors. There were also the ones who saw friends and screamed their names from meters away. There were the ones who wanted everyone else to know about their job and the millions they made or the important people they drank and dined with most of which was empty talk. Most passengers preferred to sit quiet or were engaged in soft meaningful conversations and respected fellow passengers.

Seven and half hours after takeoff, the plane landed in Malabo, Equatorial Guinea. There was a loud applause once the plane touched the tarmac. Some passengers, mostly Europeans or Americans, were taken aback and looked around hoping to see a performer, perhaps a Rihanna, on the plane but soon understood the reason for the cheers.

Some passengers got off the plane in Malabo. The flight from Malabo to Douala was less than one hour. The plane touched down in Douala to another thunderous round of applause.

The air was hot and humid in this coastal city. Jessica began sweating the moment she got off the plane. The chaos at take off in France paled in comparison to what awaited them at the baggage claim area and the airport exit.

Getting through immigration was relatively easy. She had remembered to take malaria prophylaxis but had overlooked vaccines. She took a yellow fever vaccine on the spot irrespective of the fact that protection would kick in long after she had left the country.

The customs officers were more difficult to deal with. One dug into Jessica's luggage searching for anything that could fetch him "custom duty" or a bribe. At the same time, she was surrounded by thugs parading as helpers. Once the customs officer finished ransacking her luggage, Jessica found herself in a tug of war with a thug pulling on her suitcase. She was convinced that her luggage would disappear if it got out of her site.

After receiving what he wanted, the customs officer shoved away the stubborn baggage grabber and escorted Jessica to a taxi.

She spent the night at a descent hotel a short distance from the airport. In the morning, she ate breakfast at the hotel and hired a taxi to the bus station. The bus station was almost as rowdy as the airport arrival terminal. People of all ages had merchandise on their heads and shouted out what could be considered advertisement for their products.

Jessica noticed the young girls, average age about 10 years, selling roasted peanuts, bread, bananas, fried meat or anything you could think of. At a similar age, Jessica was inseparable from her video games and Barbie dolls. Same age in Cameroon, these kids had a full time job selling small merchandise. Jessica appreciated how blessed she was to have been born in America. Doing basic household chores was considered punishment. Her parents were considered mean for making her do them. She would throw an anger tantrum and say how she hated her parents for asking her to do stuff. This is not fair, she would say. Now she was reconsidering what fairness really meant.

However, these girls in Douala seemed happy standing in the hot sun, chanting their well-rehearsed marketing song and receiving insults with a shrug of the shoulders. As Jessica would later learn, these girls were also exposed to dangers.

Sexual predators occasionally lured the girls into their homes, bought all their merchandise and then had their way with them. A quick sell and an early return home was usually a red flag. However, this was overshadowed by the good money; parents refrained from asking many questions, rather preparing more merchandise for another trip to the bus stop. These perverts often bragged to their friends about their acts. These girls always returned home, but occasionally, some disappeared never to be found. Yet parents had no choice but to keep sending children out to sell.

The bus ride to her father's place of birth in Bamenda was interesting. The bus left with a full load of passengers. As soon as they got out of the station, the driver's assistant placed wooden stools in the center of the bus. These so called attachment seats were used for extra passengers picked up along the way. The fare from these passengers was for the driver, his assistant and the police. In case of an emergency, all passengers would have been trapped by these extra seats and cargo.

Jessica was relieved when the bus pulled into the station in Bamenda. She was scared and suspicious of anyone who approached her. With her father's doctrine at the back of her mind, everyone was a potential kidnapper. It did not help that the people helping with luggage, the truck pushers and the motor cycle riders were dressed in dirty outfits that collectively passed for rags.

Eventually, Jessica overcame her fears and inquired her way to her father's home. The house matched the description she had received. The little kids playing in the dust looked vaguely familiar. Soon she was surrounded by an inquisitive crowd of kids. This happened so fast she became afraid, wondering if the kidnappers her father talked about might come in small sizes; kids napping adults, not the other way around, she thought.

She was about to scream when a woman, about her mother's age, emerged from a smaller building attached to the main house. She would later learn the smaller building was the kitchen for cooking with wood or charcoal. The woman shouted at the kids to move back, telling them to stop acting like they had never seen a white person. Jessica's mother was white and being mixed race, with very light skin, qualified her as a white person in most places in Cameroon.

"*Ma pikin, who you de find?*" asked the woman in Pidgin English?"

Jessica looked confused. A smart kid knew exactly what was happening.

"*Mamie dis one na sarah, she no de understand pidgin*" the boy said and volunteered his services as an interpreter, translating from pidgin to English and vice versa. Needless to say a lot of information was lost in translation. However, the main message went through.

Jessica told her she was looking for Mr. Chefon Mola's relatives. The kids laughed considering the name funny and were immediately hushed by the woman. Jessica was told no Mola lived in that neighborhood; it was common to know almost everyone in town, let alone the neighborhood. The woman made sure Jessica was in the right town.

Jessica was convinced Bamenda was the right place but decided to go rest in a hotel and plan the next strategy. She had come very far and was determined to get some results.

Jessica thanked the woman and walked away while contemplating her next strategy. She had to exhaust all options.

The previous night in her hotel, she had heard a radio station reading numerous announcements late in the night. Many of them had been death announcements and she had wondered if there was an epidemic in some part of the country. Maybe a radio announcement was a common way of communication here; the third world twitter, Facebook or what have you. In America, she would have sent out a twit or a Facebook post and gotten responses within the hour.

She decided to locate the nearest radio station, submit an announcement requesting to be contacted by anyone with any knowledge of Chefon Mola. *Great idea*, she concluded.

Oh no, not so great, it would just invite those kidnappers to her hotel, she concluded on second thought. Then she heard the young interpreter behind her.

The woman had sent him to get Jessica. She wanted to see a picture of this Chefon Mola because, despite her American accent, she had sensed something familiar in Jessica's voice. Yes Americans have an accent; in fact everybody has an accent. An American in Britain has an accent, a British, an Australian, a French or a Spaniard in America has an accent. Some accents are celebrated, others are despised, but we all have them.

"*I fit see picture for this Mola Chefon?*" the woman requested.

Jessica was disappointed she had not thought of it herself. *I am American, I should be smarter than her*, she thought. She looked through pictures on her phone and showed the woman her father's most recent picture.

The expression on the woman's face was telling.

"*No be Befe Mboma this?*" She said as she showed the picture to the interpreter boy?"

The boy concurred.

"*Ma pikin, come inside house, dis story long, time short. We no fit talk dis one up up*" the woman said, as they entered the living room. "*Ma name na Angelina. Wetin be your own name?*"

"My name is Jessica, Jessica Mola."

Jessica had understood the concept of Pidgin English. She could fill in the blanks and get the message without needing an interpreter. With a careful choice of words, she could also communicate her message to Angelina.

"*You say who be dis man for you?*" Angelina asked, wanting to know how Jessica was related to the man in the picture.

"He is my father" Jessica replied.

"*Father? You mean say na your papa? He marry your mamie? Dis man get woman for America? I be know say dis woman wrapper not fit tie ye skin but for go marry then born pikin. Dis one pass mark. Mboma don kill me o*" she rambled. Her hands went from grabbing her head, chest, hips, back to her head, accompanied by feet movement like in a matching band. Jessica had seen other Cameroonian women do this. It meant they were either in distress or very angry.

Jessica waited for Angelina to calm down before answering her questions.

"Yes he is married, to my mother."

Angelina sat down besides Jessica. They compared notes to ensure they were talking about the same person. The times he had visited Cameroon, the length of stay, and the things he brought all matched. The pictures on the wall also confirmed the facts. Yes, Befe Mboma and Chefon Mola was one and the same person.

Jessica felt her next question was pointless but wanted to confirm anyway.

"Who is he to you?" she asked.

"*Na ma husband o. He marry me before he go America. We get four pikin them*" Angelina replied, confirming that Mola was indeed her husband and together they had four children.

"I can't believe this. So this is what it was all about. There are no kidnappers, there is no ransom! It was all designed to hide his double life" Jessica ranted.

"Sorry ma pikin. No vex with me now. I no do any ting wrong. All dis trouble na Mboma causam no" Angelina said apologetically.

"No, I am not mad at you. I am mad at my dad. He lied to me, - to us -, all these years" Jessica said.

"Ma pikin, no craze o. I hear say when American craze he de use gun shoot people. I just tell you my true true" Angelina pleaded with her; fearing that by mad Jessica meant she was developing a mental illness; based on the stereotype about Americans, she might go for a gun and start shooting at people.

"No, I am not insane mad, I am angry mad. It means I am very angry. I will not shoot anyone. I don't own a gun."

At that point she realized the line between extreme anger and insanity was very thin. If her father had been there, it would have taken just one wrong word to turn her into a raving maniac, some sort of insanity. Who knew what could have resulted from that emotional state. The traditional machete hanging on the living room wall would have been as effective as a gun.

"Okay, ma pikin, just rest small, your heart go cool, then we fit continue de story", Angelina urged Jessica to calm down.

Jessica took a deep breath and leaned back in her seat. "Why are you not as mad as I am? Did you know about this all along?" she asked.

Angelina reminded Jessica the earlier dance and hand gestures were a display of extreme anger. She was angry quite alright, but she had endured a lot from Mboma and had learned to restrain her anger when it came to his deeds. It wasn't all that surprising that he had gotten married in the USA. While in Cameroon, he had numerous mistresses. Angelina knew all about his cheating, but stayed with him, proudly announcing that she was the woman of the house while the other women only had him part time. She would have been ok with polygamy as long as she received the respect of wife number one. Many had attributed her naïveté to a lack of formal education, the same reason, they said, Mboma had not taken her to the USA.

Jessica's anger slowly dissipated and she began to enjoy the rest of her stay with her newly discovered family. Word got out about her and numerous visitors arrived to see this American with roots to their extended family. She stopped seeing potential kidnappers in everybody and began seeing friendly company. They all agreed to keep her visit secret should her father call them.

There was a genuine connection between Angelina and Jessica. When Angelina referred to her as *my pikin* (my child) it felt natural and genuine.

Jessica's step siblings were sad to see her brief visit come to an end. They all wanted to go to the airport but Angelina nominated Tom, her eldest son to accompany Jessica to the airport. They took the same bus line that brought Jessica to Bamenda.

This time police stopped the bus halfway into the journey and asked passengers for personal identification. These were inspected and returned to most passengers.

Jessica's American passport generated some excitement and was taken to the police boss sitting in a make shift office at the road side. Moments later, a police officer came and asked Tom if he was related to Jessica. When Tom answered to the affirmative, his national identity card was taken from him again.

The police went on to stop other vehicles and went through their routine while the boss sat in the hut drinking beer, giving instructions, interrogating passengers who came to retrieve their identification, while at the same time keeping an eye on his men so that they didn't pocket any money they collected. There was a specific bag strapped around their waist into which money collected from passengers and drivers went.

Ten minutes went by and the passengers in Jessica's bus began to scream at her. They wanted her to go "*settle*" the police, "*settle*" being a politically correct word for bribe.

The bus driver went over to negotiate but made no progress. They wanted the American and her relative to come see the police boss. The "*settlement*" was going to be in dollars and it had to be big or the bus would be delayed indefinitely. These traffic police had found something "wrong" with Jessica's visa that the trained immigration officers at the airport had missed. A fee was required for the passport to be released.

A junior police officer seemed concerned that delaying a law abiding American was dangerous.

"Sir, this American can call her embassy and that will be trouble for us. Maybe we should let them go" the officer was overheard telling his boss.

"Don't worry about that. We have Tom for insurance. We can make up a story around him and tie the American in." The police boss had it all figured out.

"How are we going to do that, sir?" the concerned officer asked.

"Use your pawpaw head to think my friend" the boss said to the amusement of the other officers. "You understand pawpaw head right? When a pawpaw is cut all you see inside are a few seeds in an almost empty cavity." The boss was obviously intoxicated. "Anyway, to answer your question, we still have that Indian hemp we confiscated from those criminals. We can plant it into Tom's bag and even Mr. Pawpaw head can figure out the rest" the boss continued, apparently pleased with himself.

The uproar from passengers in Jessica's bus was getting louder and almost out of control.

"Why are you so selfish, white woman? Go give them a few dollars and relieve us all of this trouble" one passenger screamed.

"I have business to do in Douala and you are delaying me here. Do something" another passenger added.

Tom tried to intervene. "It is not her fault. Blame the police. Our documents are in order but they want money from us. Is that a good thing?"

"Oh please, cut that crap. Why are you talking as if you are not from here? You know the system, they stop you, you *settle* and everybody goes. No quarrels, no delays. It is that simple" another passenger vented at Tom.

A few passengers supported Tom and said they were willing to spend the whole day at that check point. They said it might take an American passenger to shine a spotlight on this police harassment and corruption.

Another passenger disagreed strongly with the apparent reliance on the American.

"There you go again, cowardly Cameroonians. You all sit and wait for Americans to come solve your problems. Why can't we take action, why can't we do something for ourselves? We sit around drinking beer, talking big and complaining. If I go out there to confront these thieves in uniform, will any of you support me?" He paused for an answer and got none. "You see. The Arab spring could have easily been the African spring, but south of the Sahara, we are all selfish cowards, waiting for Americans to shine the light on our issues. If you think America can ever bypass France to intervene in this country, you are probably from another planet. We are still a colony, France's sphere of influence" the angry passenger continued.

"*Shidon for down, over sabbe. Wetin you think say you one fit do. Mberreh go frap your lass dat your mouth go shut up*" another passenger said, advising him to sit down and shut his mouth. Confronting the police by himself would only result in severe torture and nothing else.

"That is exactly what I am talking about" the activist passenger said in resignation.

Tempers continued to rise and a battle was brewing between the two camps engaged in a shouting match.

"*Go settle them make we go*" one grouped screamed.

"*No give them anyting, na tief people*" the other camp countered.

Jessica had seen enough. She beckoned the driver and handed him $10 for the police in exchange for her passport and Tom's national identity card.

The rest of the trip to the airport went without any major incident.

The return flight was on schedule. Tom promised to stay at the airport until the plane took off.

Since Jessica did not have much luggage, her check in was relatively quick. Her only problem was that she had no local currency left for airport tax. She had to pay in dollars which ended up being in excess of the regular amount. The officer in charge had no change although she had dollar bills sticking out of her wallet.

The return flight went from Douala to Paris and then Paris to Hartford.

She got more questions entering the USA than she got leaving Cameroon. The immigration agent wanted to know why she had gone to Cameroon, who she travelled with, where she stayed, what she had brought back. Her luggage was searched thoroughly. It was like the arrival in Douala without the heat, chaos and the thugs. She breathed a sigh of relief when she was finally let go.

Jessica could not wait to confront her father with the wealth of information she had gathered. Her mother was excited to see her but dad seemed indifferent. After talking with her mother for a couple of hours, Jessica pulled her father aside for a talk.

"When were you going to tell us, dad? Jessica asked.

"Tell you what?" dad asked.

"The other family – wife, children and grandchildren" Jessica continued.

"What has gotten into you? Were you drugged in Mexico or what?" dad asked, looking perplexed.

"FYI …" Jessica said, twisting her neck and rotating her head for emphasis. "I did not go to Mexico. I went to Cameroon."

"Oh, so you lied to us. Did your mother know about this?"

"Look who is talking about lies. You expect truth from me! Hypocrisy that is what it is. I guess lying is in the genes I got from you, Mr. Mboma!"

Dad was cornered. He decided to come clean. It would have been foolish to keep arguing.

"Calm down Jess. We really have to talk, don't we" dad said.

"You are damn right we have to talk. That is what I have been trying to do."

"There is an African proverb that you can hide your nakedness from everyone but the toilet will always see it. The truth cannot be buried, like Jesus, it will always resurrect and come back to stare you in the face. I will tell you everything" dad rambled.

"I don't get the analogy. Who is the toilet here?" Jessica asked. "Anyway, I am anxiously waiting for your story, your version of truth."

"I am still your father you know. There is also an African proverb that the shoulder can never grow taller than the head."

"I have had enough of your proverbs already. My patience is running thin. If you are slowly laying the foundation for more lies, I can assure you it will not work."

"I will not hold back anything, I assure you. Freezer or oven, it makes no difference to a dead chicken" dad said, as he opened the bottle of beer he had brought with him. He longed for something stronger than beer, like vodka, to calm his nerves. This could be the end of life as he knew it.

Mola aka Mboma's story in his own words

I worked for the government in Cameroon. I was the treasurer general in my province so I had direct access to and controlled a lot of cash. The post came with a lot of prestige, and as time went on, I adopted an expensive lifestyle, far beyond my means.

I had many girlfriends, most of them university students, patronized the most expensive restaurants, and got myself a new car. However, my salary was not big enough for someone who controlled so much money.

The mention of girlfriends stirred some compassion for Angelina in Jessica.

"Did Angelina ever confront you about the many women and your extravagance?" Jessica asked.

Not with any conviction. She was happy to be married to an educated man with a lot of influence and feared losing that perceived privilege.

"Sorry to interrupt. An extravagant lifestyle, little income, access to state cash - a recipe for disaster right!"

You are right. I was paying for this with state money. I succeeded in hiding my stealing from state auditors year after year. They always accepted my gifts before every audit, which in a way clouded their judgment.

I became increasingly reckless and soon the deficit was obvious. There was no money to pay pensioners, government bills and salaries for casual workers. Subordinates began to complain, and petitioned the governor who in turn referred the matter to the minister of finance. The governor could not take direct action because he had unjustifiably requested cash from the treasury on many occasions. He had requested the largest amount during a presidential campaign, when Lionman was up for reelection. Actually it had been an ultimatum, not a request. He had summoned me to his office to deliver it in person.

"I need one million francs from you for the presidential campaign" the governor had said. "I have to show my loyalty and support by sending in a descent amount of money to the central committee of the party."

I told him there was no such amount of money floating around in the treasury.

"We all have to protect our jobs, you know. You have to find a way of coming up with that money, I guess. I am sure you value your job and want to stay in that position after the elections" the governor said.

I wondered why he was so certain Lionman would be reelected. He seemed to read my mind.

"The election is just a formality, a way to fool donor countries and United Nation bodies that we are democratic. We have systems in place to rig the elections, anyway" he continued.

I told him people would revolt if their votes were stolen.

"You really don't value your job, do you? On whose side are you anyway?" he asked with a stern look. "By the way, people can revolt all they want. Lionman will be president for as long as he wants. All he needs to do is remain faithful to and defend French interest in Cameroon. If he doesn't raise a finger against this king maker, and continues to publicly distinguish himself from other African leaders as the best French puppet aka *meilleur eleve*, he will be fine. The Abakwa bookseller's strong anti-France position has already put him out of contention for the presidency. They would rather groom Junior Lion to succeed his father than let their enemy run this country.

And guess what else, Lionman can always count on the fact that the ordinary citizen will drown his frustration in beer and palm wine and take no action, no matter what he does. He is also exploiting their tribalism and evil feelings against each other and is confident they can never form a united front to fight his injustice and corruption. Things will change in this country the day people forgo alcohol and greed and form a united front against the corruption and injustice of a regime that I am forced to be part of."

I wondered why we had to contribute campaign money when the election was already decided. He read my mind again.

"I told you already. Our contribution is a sign of loyalty. Every provincial delegate and senior government official is sending money to my office. Your amount is highest but you control the most money in the province. I don't want to be outdone by the other governors, so go figure out something as soon as possible" he concluded.

I went back to my office and cooked the books to come up with the money he wanted. This also emboldened me to steal even more for myself. The one million francs was already on my neck anyway. I knew of colleagues who had given out money under similar circumstances but were later arrested for embezzlement.

With the ballooning deficit and the petitions from my staff, the minister of finance decided to set up a special commission to come investigate my treasury. The commission was composed of politicians, none of them auditors, to come do the job of auditors. A commission was usually a forum to compensate political allies with trips and per diems. They usually had their results before embarking on their mission.

In my case, it had already been concluded that I was guilty. They had to come figure out a monetary value for my corruption.

As is often the case with most corrupt officials in the provinces, I had an insider in the ministry of finance. My insider tipped me off about the impending investigation and I sprang into action immediately. I knew I could not escape prison if I remained in the country.

I got a letter of invitation from my friend and obtained a visitor's visa for the USA. It was faster and less complicated to get a US visa at the time. All I needed was proof of employment in Cameroon.

For some reason the minister also changed his mind, requesting that I should be arrested sooner. Again my insider leaked this to me.

With the noose tightening on me, I decided on an immediate escape. Needless to say, I took more state money with me as I ran away from the law. There is an African proverb that, if you choose to eat a frog, you better go for the fattest one possible.

On the run

I hired a car from Bamenda to Ekok via Mamfe. The driver was very experienced and very familiar with the route. I gave him extra money for any potential police troubles and urged him to go as fast as he could. This guy knew his way around potholes and gutters on the roads.

His sound system was really loud and his choice of music would have been annoying otherwise. However, I was too preoccupied with my plans and the uncertainties that lay ahead to care about what he listened to.

There were many police check points along the way and we stopped at all of them. At the ones close to Bamenda, the officers recognized me. Some of them had dealings with my office and remembered the 10 to 50% they had to loss in order to get whatever money they came to collect. However, they did not see this encounter as a payback opportunity. They saw it as an opportunity to sow a seed that would probably yield a good harvest when next they came to the treasury. They let my driver go, making it clear that it was out of respect for the big man, - me-, that they chose not to check his papers. Checking papers meant asking for money. They clearly did not know that I was a fugitive on the run.

At the other checkpoints, my driver readily satisfied the police by putting money in a folder that carried his documents. This made the journey fast. We got to Ekok, the last village before Nigeria, late afternoon.

I converted some money from CFA Francs to the Nigerian Naira, enough to cover my expenses all the way to Lagos, barring any unforeseen expenses.

I was very nervous, looking over my shoulder every few minutes. I wanted to cross the border as soon as possible, be out of the country before anybody knew I was on the run.

A young man approached me to find out if I needed help crossing the border into Nigeria. His name was Jimmy. He had seen me obtain the Naira, which usually signaled a trip to Nigeria. He pitched his experience to me in a well-rehearsed speech, while at the same time pointing out the dangers of trying to do it by myself. I could not agree with him more for I knew how harsh it could get on the other side of the border.

"We can arrange a fee for my services on the other side of the border. I will make sure you are not disturbed by the immigration and customs. All you have to do is give me some money and your passport once you are ready to cross. I assure you, I will take good care of you" Jimmy said. "You can deal with the Cameroon side yourself."

With money hidden all over my body and my luggage, I certainly needed all the help available to go across the border. I could not let anybody search me because that would have raised alarm bells. Even if I succeeded to proceed with most of the cash after that, they would most probably have put robbers on my tail.

I promised Jimmy extra money if all went according to plan, an extra incentive for him to bring out his "A" game.

Time to start the border crossing process, I walked nervously into the Cameroon customs and immigration office, presented my passport to an immigration officer, told him I was going to Calabar to visit my sick brother and waited for him to put the exit stamp in my passport, no questions asked. Instead he leaned back in his seat and started flipping through my passport. The recently acquired USA visa caught his attention and he asked me when I was planning to visit the USA. In two months, I said and could tell he did not believe me.

My heart skipped a beat when he got up and went to the police chief's office. Minutes later I was invited into the chief's office. We had met at meetings. He was surprised to see me there. We talked briefly but I could tell he was preoccupied. He excused himself to make an important call.

"Is the governor in the office?" the chief asked when the phone was answered.

"He is in an important meeting right now? When is the meeting going to end? In 2 hours? Okay. No, it is not urgent. I just wanted to confirm something with him. Yes it can wait."

Then he hung up. My heart was pounding and sweat ran down my armpits like a tiny stream. I struggled to stay calm.

"When are you coming back?" the chief asked me.

"In two to three days" I said.

"And when do you plan to visit America?" he asked.

"In two months' time" I replied.

"What takes you to America?" he asked.

"I will be visiting my friend. He is getting married and I will be the best man" I lied.

He personally stamped my passport and handed it over to me.

"Have a safe trip. Please, make sure you see me on your way back. It is important" he said.

He apparently knew what was going on in my office but did not have sufficient information to stop me from leaving the country. Had he spoken to the governor I would have been arrested on the spot. I left as fast as I could.

I spotted Jimmy talking with his fellow border crossing facilitators. It was an animated conversation about a recent soccer game that Cameroon had lost to Nigeria. A loss in soccer was usually bad news for both the government and the general public. The government had come to rely on the euphoria that came with a victory to quickly introduce changes that would otherwise have elicited some degree of public outcry. On the other hand, a loss had the potential of pushing passionate fans into the streets, especially if they strongly disagreed with the coach's player selection; or as was often the case, if the government overruled the coach. Everyone usually had an opinion about who should be fired from the team. On this particular occasion, Jimmy thought the goal keeper was to blame and wished the team had used the other professional keeper. Someone disagreed and an argument ensued. He gestured for me to wait.

"Thomas is old. We should not pick our goalies based on past glory, okay. Jack is young and skilled and should be our number one keeper any time, any day" Jimmy yelled at his friends.

"It wasn't Thomas' fault. I blame the defense. The coach brought in so called professionals but these are bench warmers in Europe. With such a useless defense Jack could not have stopped that goal from going in. Thomas is not living on past glory, he has relevant experience to be number one" a man yelled back.

"You don't know anything. Anthony has more experience than Thomas, okay. But they are both old, Jack is the man" Jimmy continued. Jimmy wanted to win this argument before attending to me but changed his mind when another facilitator approached me.

"Leave him alone" Jimmy yelled. "He is mine. Learn to respect your seniors" he continued, shoving his competition on the shoulder.

At that point I wondered if I had made the right decision. Jimmy looked like potential trouble. However, there was no backing out. I did not want to elicit from him the kind of reaction I had just witnessed and also did not want to attract any more police attention.

I quickly gave Jimmy the money he requested and handed him my passport. We walked the short distance to the banks of the Cross River that serves as part of the boundary between Cameroon and Nigeria. We stepped on the high suspension bridge that links the two countries. I looked back to bid farewell to my beloved country and then turned my attention to what lay ahead.

Half way across, I made the mistake of looking down into the river and was frightened by the high bridge. Then I recalled a horror story about a student who had attempted to escape from Nigerian customs and immigration officers by holding unto iron rods under the bridge and navigating across the bridge. He had been spotted by an officer. Instead of helping him from under the bridge, the officer had used a stick to poke at the student's hands, to make him fall into the river. The horrified student had eventually surrendered and fallen into the river. Fortunately his injuries had not been life threatening and he had made it out of the river on the Cameroonian side.

I quickened my steps, wanting to be off the bridge as soon as possible. However, once off the bridge, we were welcome by a stern looking officer. His hand hovered menacingly over a gun strapped around his waist as he directed us into the Mfun customs and immigration office.

Once inside it reminded me of the stories I had heard from Cameroonians who went to university in Nigeria.

There were immigration and custom officers sitting in clusters behind desks along the four walls of the outer room. Each cluster of officers looked at each passport, immunization records and other documents. Once a levy was paid, the documents were passed to the next group of officers who went through the same ritual. Once the documents completed the rounds of the outer office, the inner room was next. This was the most important room. The stamp that authorized visitors to proceed resided in this room. This was also the most expensive stop, commensurate with its importance in deciding the fate of visitors.

Jimmy took care of the outer office in a breeze. The inner office turned out to be more difficult. The boss insisted on seeing me in person. He had seen the American visa and was convinced I was running away from something in my country. He seemed to see right through my plans. He just knew I was on my way to America.

"I know you are not going back to Cameroon. Can you tell me why you are leaving through Nigeria?" the boss asked me.

"I will go back to my country. I am just visiting my brother for two days" I lied again.

"That is not true. I can send you back to face justice, you know" the boss said. "But there is an easy way for both of us. Your man here has given me something but I think it should be more. Make it big and I will let you go, okay."

Jimmy asked to talk with me alone. He wanted to know if what the officer had said was true. I flatly refused but gave him more money, enough to satisfy the officer.

I was relieved when Jimmy came back with my passport and declared part one solved. There were other checkpoints ahead but these ones were less complicated, he said.

I could understand why most Cameroonian students returning to Nigeria had sleepless nights prior to their trips. It could be a traumatizing experience for those who didn't have enough money to give these officers. Some students were detained when they could not satisfy these demands. Nigerians travelling to Cameroon on business suffered the same fate in the hands of the Cameroonian authorities. The difference, however, was that what the Nigerians gave as bribe was paid back by the Cameroonian customers who paid extra for any merchandise the Nigerians sold.

Jimmy did a great job at the other checkpoints. It was night by the time we cleared the last check point. He accompanied me to a hotel in Ikom, where I gave him extra money, honoring my earlier promise. He was delighted and offered to help me on my way back to Cameroon if I told him precisely when I planned to return. *Sorry sucker, I am not going back to Cameroon anytime soon,* I said to myself.

I barely slept that night. The next day I travelled to Calabar where I converted some of my CFA Francs to US dollars at a *bureau d'echange*. Next I booked a flight for the USA, taking off from Lagos and then a local flight from Calabar to Lagos. I was fortunate to get on these flights, even though they were more expensive than normal.

Getting on the US bound flight was less complicated than I anticipated. I was asked the routine questions for that era.

"The US authorities actually let you on the flight that easily? Nobody was told you were a fugitive? The Cameroonian government did not inform Interpol about you?" Jessica asked, surprised.

African governments didn't share information about fugitives. The US gathered its own information almost independently. Sometimes, tip offs about criminals and dangerous people were not taken seriously. That is still true today, in a way, even with all the hype about terrorism.

"The good old days, I guess. Post underwear bomber, they would have vetted you and denied you entry into the US. You would probably be somewhere in Lagos today" Jessica said.

Yes you are right, the good old days indeed. Not like today, when the person sitting next to you on the plane is a suspect until you get out of the plane alive; conspicuous luggage deserves special attention; while at the same time it is a crime to travel without or with small baggage. We all need to carry big baggage to prove that we are sane, so much attention to physical baggage, ignoring mental baggage and access to guns which also creates potential terrorists.

The police were at my house to arrest me the next day after I left Cameroon. When they could not locate me, Angelina was arrested in my place and kept in prison for some days. She was tortured for information but she had none for the police. I had left her in the dark about my plans.

Frustrated, the police went after the women I was housing around town, especially the conspicuous ones who kept me company around town and on official missions to other towns. These ones had more questions than answers for the police. Beauty and flirtation saved them from the police torture and earned them a quick release from the police station.

My parting gift for my family and friends was nothing less than confusion, torture and desperation.

I arrived the USA and stayed with the same friend who had provided me with the invitation letter. My friend had no job at the time and relied solely on social welfare. His apartment was a mess and his fridge was almost empty. He lived on junk food and beer. I guess I was given a visa on my own strength. If he had been required to show evidence that he could support a guest, I would not have received a visa.

I bought food and supplies for both of us. Since I was a descent cook, I started making meals for both of us. My friend began to appreciate my coming to America. He said I was destined for a better life in the USA but felt sad for the way I had left my family.

I ran out of money within a couple of months. My friend's social welfare cheque could not take care of two people. I needed to start working immediately.

However, my visitor's visa did not permit me to work in the USA. Since my friend wasn't working, he decided to lend me his identity for the purpose of work. He was happy to let me work and take care of both of us, so I adopted his identity for work. That is how my journey to becoming Chefon Mola began.

We had an arrangement; he spent part of the money I made. Then he became sick. All that time I thought he was lazy, a medical condition had been contributing to his reluctance to work. He did not know it either.

His condition depreciated rapidly and he decided to go back to Cameroon. A strange choice at the time considering he could have gotten better medical attention in the USA. However, come to think of it, without a good medical insurance in this country, you are almost worse off than an average person in a third world country. The money I sent to him every month went a long way in Cameroon. He sought the best medical care, got affordable medication from licensed pharmacies and paid for two maids, a luxury I could not afford in this part of the world.

Unfortunately, the terminal illness took his life eventually and from that time on there was only one Chefon Mola alive – me.

At the beginning, it was very difficult to be Chefon Mola full time. I answered to Mola at work and continued to be Mboma to other Cameroonians who knew me. The most awkward moments were when I met colleagues while in the company of other Cameroonians. They would call me Mola and the Cameroonians would look around, confused and almost scared that my colleagues were seeing Mola's ghost. I would respond and later explain to my fellow Cameroonians that it was a mix up because we all looked the same to white people.

Then I gradually started avoiding Cameroonians.

As years went by, being Mola became so natural. I introduced myself as Mola to everybody.

"So you stole his identity?" Jessica asked.

No, I did not steal his identity. It was an identity relay; he handed me his identity and made a smooth transition possible.

"How did a dead man facilitate a smooth transition?" Jessica asked, confused.

He sent his documents to me from Cameroon before passing away. These came along with a letter that made his wishes clear. I guess we could call it his will with me as the sole beneficiary. The letter read as follows:

Dear friend,

This might be my last letter to you. My doctor says I have only a few days to live.

I want to thank you for all your help. You changed my life the day you arrived the USA; the cleaning, the cooking and especially my regular portion of your salary. You have faithfully respected our arrangement. If not for this illness, I would have lived like a king in this country. Even with the regular therapy and the fatigue, I still found time to go to the Limbe beach on a regular basis. Because of you, my life has been less painful than it would have been otherwise.

As a token of appreciation, I am sending all my documents and certificates to you. I believe these will help you fully become me, if you so desire. As you know, I have no siblings or relatives that will be snooping around after I go.

I wish you all the best. I hope you can start visiting your family in Cameroon soon.

Your friend
Chefon.

"When did you start visiting Cameroon?" Jessica asked.

Ten years after my escape. However, my family knew where I was two months after I escaped.

"Why weren't you arrested when you visited Cameroon?" Jessica probed.

The government and the police had long forgotten about me. That is how easy it is for grand thieves to escape prosecution in my country. All it takes is a few years out of the country and you can return to live lavishly on the ill-gotten wealth. You can become a vocal supporter of the ruling party to reenter their good books.

Besides I entered the country as Chefon Mola.

"How did you get a passport as Mola?"

Again I thank the good old days. I had all of my friend's documents including his birth certificate. I don't know how but I succeeded in getting American citizenship as Chefon Mola. I can only guess they did not compare my finger prints with the original documents in file; they probably assumed the photo discrepancy was due to age or perhaps mine was just one rare case that slipped through the cracks. In today's digitalized world, I would have been caught.

As a citizen, it was easy to obtain an American passport. Once in Cameroon, I reverted to my original identity as Befe Mboma. I always kept a low profile. My brief visits were worthwhile.

"You missed your children and grandchildren, I guess" Jessica inquired.

Yes, especially the grandchildren. There is something special about being a grandfather that turns an irresponsible lying jerk like me into someone with a semblance of responsibility.

"I recognized them once I saw them. I now understand why all those pictures on the fridge were so important to you. The poor kids you sponsored through a local organization were actually your grandchildren. Why did you not just send money directly to them?" Jessica asked.

I don't know. That was probably me pushing the limits again. My kinds of jobs did not help. Fraud, lies and cheating seem to be more of an addiction than we know. The car salesman lies to you with a straight face day in day out and that becomes part of his life; I bet he takes the lying home with him at the end of the day. The insurance sales person lies to you about the extent of your coverage and the ease with which your claim will be paid and you think the lies disappear once they start doing other things? Trained to lie at work means trained to lie in life. The truth is, I now seem to thrive on lies since my whole life here in the USA has been a lie anyway.

"How did Angelina not know you were traveling as Chefon Mola and not Mboma? Didn't she look at your passport, or your flight ticket or something?"

I hid all my documents the moment I got into the house. She was contented with seeing me and seldom asked any questions.

"Does my mother know about this?" Jessica asked.

No. She knows the Mola that I allowed her to know and nothing about Mboma.

"That is a creepy story dad. I don't know who you are anymore? Nobody knows who you are. You are terrible. Now I know more than I can handle and it is my mother's turn to learn about the stranger she married. I will grant you the honor of telling her yourself" Jessica said.

"Please don't do that to your mother. She is not well so she might not handle this" Mola pleaded.

"I am sure she can handle it" Jessica insisted.

"Listen to me my daughter. If I may paraphrase another African proverb from the Ibo land, what an old man can see sitting down, a child cannot see even if she climbs up the tallest tree in the land. Please spare your mother the pain and heartache. I will find a better time and way to tell her" Mola continued to plead.

"Sorry, I refuse to be bamboozled by your African proverbs, whatever their meaning. I will not let this lie persist for another day. No, not on my watch" Jessica said emphatically and called her mother.

"Mom, dad has something very important to tell you. Come quickly before he changes his mind."

Pa Mola repeated his story to his American wife. Ellen seemed frozen in her seat throughout the story.

"I knew you were weird and creepy the very first day I met you" Ellen said. "I should have trusted my judgment at that time and stayed away from you. However, I did not know you were capable of all these. You lied to me, cheated on your first wife and committed identity theft; now I know you are capable of anything. From what I know now, I won't be surprised if you poisoned your friend in order to inherit his identity. You better start considering which lawyer will defend you because I am calling the police right now."

It was Mola's turn to freeze. He sat motionless and almost expressionless; almost like an embalmed corpse. As Ellen got up to reach for the phone, he finally attempted to speak but it came out as a whisper.

"Ellen, please don't. It will destroy my life, our lives. I am very sorry for lying to you" Mola said.

"Don't talk to me. Open your mouth again and I will shove a long knife down your throat." Ellen yelled at him for the very first time since they knew each other. It was a sound that surprised Mola, Jessica and even Ellen herself.

Ellen held on to the edge of her seat for a few minutes. Her eyes seemed to slowly sweep across the room, as if taking in the scene for one last time. She looked at the African carvings on the wall, then at the traditional machete in a leather casing, before letting her eyes drift over to the various pictures that had immortalized some of the memorable events in their lives. Her eyes then went to Jessica's most recent school portrait. She had commented about the portrait that if she were to die soon, she would rest in peace knowing that she raised a beautiful, strong and intelligent woman, for Jessica looked like a woman in that portrait. Finally she turned away from the portrait to look at Jessica, as if asking herself why she was looking at a picture while the person was right there to admire.

Then Jessica noticed something was terribly wrong. Ellen suddenly looked very pale.

She was on medication for a chronic heart condition and usually suffered dizzy spells shortly after taking her medicines. She had taken her medication earlier in the day. However, the stress induced by Mola's story and the energy expended in yelling at her husband were bad for her ailing heart.

"My daughter, I am feeling sick. I think I am going to faint. Can you help me to my room please?"

Jessica came to her help.

"Mom, should I call the ambulance? You look horrible" Jessica asked. Mola came to help but even in her weak state, Ellen mustered enough energy to push him away. Then she fainted.

Mola called 911 while Jessica desperately tried to help Ellen. She was rushed to the hospital by ambulance.

Mola and Jessica also went to the hospital and waited anxiously outside Ellen's room. Jessica kept blaming herself for bringing this mishap to her mother. She could be heard mumbling "please God, let her live. God keep my mother alive. I will kill myself if she dies."

"Jess, she is just in severe distress. I am sure she will be fine. This hospital has some of the best doctors and I am sure they will take care of whatever it is" Mola tried to assure his daughter, though his face betrayed the doubt and worry he too felt.

"Did you say whatever it is? It is a broken heart, okay. She better live or else..." Jessica began to say but was interrupted by the doctor who had been attending to Ellen.

"How is she doc?" Mola asked.

"I am sorry sir. It was a heart attack. We did all we could but she did not make it. I am so sorry" the doctor said.

Jessica blamed herself for her mother's death. If she had not gone to Cameroon and discovered her father's double life, her mother would still be alive.

"They say ignorance is bliss. I was overcome by the desire to know my roots, to know more about my father and at what cost? At an unbearable price.....my mother..... who was the only true and honest person in my life is gone" Jessica told her father between tears. "I am scared of life, you and everyone around me. I don't know what to do."

"Jessica, it will be okay. I have not been an honest person and I am truly sorry for everything. I wish I had told your mother all about myself but I was so deep into this mess. I know it is a big ask but please trust me. I will be here for you and I will make things right" Mola pleaded.

"Dad, I don't think you know right from wrong anymore. You may need the judicial system to reset your moral compass. I should probably do what my mother wanted to do…. Call the police and fill them in about your fakery."

"Please, don't do it. I can't do much about the past but I will be an honest man from now on. Even if you no longer need me, think about the people in Cameroon who depend on me. I am sure you care about them" Mola continued pleading.

"You know what, you are right. I care about the people in Cameroon. I really connected with Angelina and my half siblings. I risk being an accomplice to your crime someday but I can risk that for the sake of the extended family. It will be hard to really respect you, though."

Jessica decided not to send the remaining parent to jail and has since lived with Pa Mola's secret. Pa Mola suffered some bouts of depression after his wife's death but has since overcome it. He has cleaned up his act but could not let go of Chefon Mola. Going forward, he has decided to be an "honest" Chefon Mola.

Albert was dumbfounded by Pa Mola's story. He had underestimated what fellow Cameroonians were capable of doing.

"If you ask me, I think Pa Mboma is a more appropriate name for that man. He looks like a python aka *mboma* that has just swallowed a goat."

Albert and Samson laughed at the joke and joined the others on the dance floor.

5

Marriages of Convenience

Albert's friends, most of whom he had not seen for a long time, either came to visit him or invited him to their homes. This was a common trend for new immigrants; the first couple of weeks after arrival, friends and acquaintances stayed in touch. It was some kind of immigration honey moon. After this period, you were on your own, only seeing your friends on rare occasions. Albert made the best of this honey moon while it lasted, sharing stories and reliving the college, university and work years with his friend.

The first visitor was Bruno. Bruno and Albert started university the same year before Bruno married his high school sweet heart, Vandoline.

Vandoline was born in the USA while her mother was visiting, which automatically made Vandoline a US citizen. She was taken to Cameroon when she was three weeks old and only came back to the US after high school.

While in the US, she stayed in touch with Bruno and they exchanged the most romantic letters and emails, keeping the flames of love alive. She visited Bruno two years after leaving Cameroon and her second visit, a year later, had been for their marriage.

The couple seemed very happy and went everywhere together. They went to the night club on Bruno's weekends off and were always hugging and kissing. They were known as the love birds while others claimed the public affection was a compensation for what was missing in the bedroom.

Suddenly, everything changed. Vandoline became mean and showed no interest in Bruno. She would push him when he attempted to hug her; the smooth kiss on the lips was replaced by a "land it on my behind Mister". Any effort by Bruno to have a descent conversation with her was either ignored or met with a one line conversation stopper.

"How did things change so fast between you and Vandoline? We admired you. You two seemed like a perfect match, a match made in heaven" Albert asked.

"It is a long story my friend. They say all that glitters is not gold, you know. It had to do with Eve's arrival to the USA" Bruno said.

"How is that?" Albert asked.

"Remember we were always a threesome the first time Vandoline came to visit in Cameroon. Eve accompanied us to every party, every friend we visited, when we went to church and even when we went to my home. Rumors began to spread that I was involved with both Eve and Vandoline" Bruno narrated.

"I remember those rumors. I remember some perverts telling you to be proud of it; that it was every young man's fantasy to be in a threesome" Albert said.

"If only they knew what was really going on. It was a love triangle, to say the least but it wasn't a typical one" Bruno continued. "You need to know Eve's story to really comprehend my situation."

Eve, like many other young Cameroonians, was desperate to come to America. Her plan was to find a white American who will eventually bring her here. She started posting her pictures and soliciting men on the internet while still in high school. She posted provocative pictures and desperate messages.

I am a young beautiful African princess looking for a white man to marry. If you are white and from America contact me through my email. I want to marry you and come to America. My country is poor and corrupt and there is no future for me here. Come rescue me and fly me away to the promise land.

Princess Eve.

Of course she got rapid replies from perverts who resided on the internet in search of easy prey. Most of them asked for explicit pictures, others asked for videos of her playing with herself and others took it even further, asking for a video of her in an act with a man. Eve sent more provocative pictures but refused to cross the line into sending videos over the internet. She had learned a lesson through her friend who had sent out videos to a man. The man had said he wanted these videos as a final confirmation that she was real before coming to marry her the following week. Once he had received these videos he stopped writing to Eve's friend. Soon afterwards these videos appeared on a porn website under the caption "desperate Cameroonian sluts."

Eve's solicitors also disappeared after getting the pictures they wanted. Frustration forced Eve to confess her online solicitations to Vandoline.

"You should have told me this long ago" Vandoline said, with a hint of disappointment. "You know I can connect you with a guy who will take you to America."

"I did not know that. Please introduce me to this guy. Who is he?" Eve asked.

"Pete Kimah. He is American and he has no girlfriend. You are pretty, he will fall for you immediately" Vandoline said. Pete was also a high school student in Cassava farms.

"Pete? No way, I cannot marry him. He is not my type" Eve said categorically.

"You want to go to America don't you? I would rather take the man I see than wait for an unknown to show up from an internet connection. All you need is access to the USA, I believe" Vandoline tried to reason with Eve.

It wasn't hard to convince Eve. "I guess you are right. I can marry and stick with him until we get to America. I can then go my way. You will be there at the time and we can....you know what I mean."

"Good. I will arrange an outing with Pete and some other friends this weekend and leave the rest to you. I know how aggressive you can be when you want something, so I am confident you will have him hooked by the end of the night" Vandoline concluded. Her words turned out to be prophetic. Eve put on quite a show and by the end of the night Pete was smitten.

After high school, Pete went to the university and Eve went to a local nursing school. He was still in love with her and she was still patiently playing along, hoping they would marry soon and move to America. But Pete was determined to get a first degree in Cameroon.

Eve completed her course while Pete still had a year of university left. She was offered a part time job at a health clinic. They got married the moment Pete graduated, and started the visa process for Eve so that both of them could move to the USA.

But shortly after the marriage, Pete began to notice some telltale signs of what lay ahead. Eve was more at ease with her male coworkers and friends than she was with him. The day after their wedding, she spent hours talking to a male friend with whom she had walked past Pete without any introduction. Pete was suddenly an invisible presence. Pete would come back from trips and barely get a hug from his new bride but when she ran into her colleagues it was hugs and loud kisses. When Pete made plans to have lunch with her, she would rather beg a colleague to take her to lunch, leaving him waiting at home.

Despite all these red flags, Pete was convinced once he took her to the USA, things would be better. He was hoping he would be the apple of her eye once in the land of the big apple. After all, he was taking her out of poverty into a life of opportunity, a land of freedom. The reward for this, Pete thought, could only be gratitude and more respect from Eve. Ironically, this freedom included the freedom to express ones sexual orientation and Pete had no control over this part of the bundle.

Eve got her visa with relative ease. They moved to America shortly thereafter, both full of hope and anticipation. Pete was hoping for a better relationship and possibly, a happily ever after for him and his wife. Eve on her part was hoping for a happy reunion with someone else.

Eve got her wish. Her friend was awaiting her arrival with great excitement and a carefully designed plan to get Pete out of the way. This included aggressive behavior and trash talk in response to anything her husband said.

Pete endured Eve's torture for months and continued to hope that things will turn around. He was gentle with her because he was so in love with his wife. However, this only made Eve more desperate. She decided to ratchet up the rhetoric and unbelievable words started pouring out of her mouth.

This finally got to Pete. The last straw came in an unexpected way. Eve was on the phone with a friend in an apparently planned conversation, designed to point out perceived flaws in Pete's physique and the fact that marrying him was a huge compromise on her part. This had the desired effect. A humiliated Pete left his apartment in search of comfort.

A mutual friend of theirs, Loveline, lived a short distance away. Pete went to Loveline because he knew that she would always listen to his troubles.

"Why are you here... without Eve?" Loveline asked.

"Guess what? My wife settled when she married me. She had always wanted a tall, handsome rich man for a husband. Look at me, am I tall? No, I am not" Pete said with a shake of the head.

"What makes you think that?" Loveline asked. "She could not have told you that."

"Oh yes she did! She was on the phone with her friend and knew I was sitting right there" Pete said.

"I am sorry to hear that. I don't think my friend meant to hurt you. You might be taking it out of context" Loveline attempted to console Pete.

"She meant everything she said. She did not find Mr. Right, this being the tall, handsome, rich and powerful man. A hero that will slay lions and trample on everything that lies in his path, a man that will be the center of attraction in the room or the crowd. And guess what? By this definition, Mr. Right will never be a one woman's man and it seems true. Mr. Right is usually selfish, arrogant, treats her badly and lets her know that other women will come running if she leaves. In my opinion, there has never been any worse misnomer in a woman's vocabulary....it should be Mr. Wrong. Mr. Right should be any man who treats her with respect, is there for her and will have time to regret losing her before another woman ever comes along. Unfortunately these guys are described as being too nice to be marriage material, except as a last resort. Anyway, whatever it is, she did not find him, so she settled for this short man. You know what that means. I am a loser....the last pick at the game. And you know what else? If she had the potential of holding on to the so called Mr. Right, she won't be stuck with me today. And now a lot makes sense to me – why some of the men fitting her description of Mr. Right still called repeatedly and wanted to meet her when they came to town and why she still flirted with them on Facebook" Pete rambled on and on.

"You are a great guy Pete. I know she loves you. I will talk to her" Loveline offered.

"No please. I have lost my self-esteem already. I don't feel like a man anymore. If you talk to her she will only bark at me and hurt me some more. I now understand why she has been so aggressive with me. I can't have a conversation with her without ending up losing a piece of my dignity. She has been working hard to reduce me into a hopeless man."

Loveline felt genuinely sorry for Pete. He was a good man and always cared for his wife. For him to be this bitter and disturbed meant his wife had pushed a sensitive button. Loveline wished she could do something to ease Pete's pain but what. Her best bet was to mediate and let them talk it over but Pete did not want that.

"You have been a wonderful husband to her Pete" Loveline said, not knowing what else to say. "You are not that short and if you ask me, I think you are very handsome. She is lucky to have you as a husband."

Pete's eyes lit up. Finally someone seemed to appreciate him. "Thank you Loveline. I think you are a beautiful woman too." Loveline looked startled and Pete immediately apologized. "Sorry, I should not be saying that to my wife's friend."

"It is okay. I know it is just a compliment and nothing more" Loveline said, trying to put up a wall in case Pete had ulterior motives. "By the way, Eve's definition of Mr. Right is not the same as mine and I believe most women will side with me. Mr. Right is not based on any physical or financial characteristics; it is a thing of the heart. There is a gut feeling that comes over everyone when they meet that right person. Unfortunately some women fight this gut feeling and chase after superficial qualities."

"Yes, yes you are right. Thank you for making me feel better though. I will go home now."

"I was about to eat dinner. I cooked some Cameroonian food and it happens to be one of your favorite. You can join me if you don't mind" Loveline offered.

"I cannot turn down an offer for a good meal. I may not even be offered any food in my home."

They had dinner together. She opened a bottle of wine Eve had given her and they drank during the meal. Their conversation slowly took a different direction after the bottle of wine. Then they made a mistake and then continued making the same mistake over and over until it began to feel right. Eve was oblivious because she was also busy in her own indiscretions.

Loveline soon learned the real reason for Eve's provocative behavior towards her husband.

"Eve is not and has never been interested in any tall, handsome men, if at all she was ever interested in men" Loveline told Pete one day.

"What do you mean? She definitely was interested in me. That is why she married me" Pete said, confused.

"Well, let's put it this way. At some point in her life she might have been interested in finding Mr. Right and perhaps went out with some men. But in reality she had Mrs. Right all along" Loveline continued to confuse Pete.

"Again, what do you mean?"

"Your dear wife has been messing around with one of her good friends. Her friend has left her husband so she can be with Eve. Is that clear to you now?" Loveline asked.

"No it is not. Are you saying my wife is...never mind. No that is not true...I mean, that is not possible" a visibly distressed Pete said incoherently.

"I am sorry Pete. I wish there was an easier way to tell you this but that is the truth. She is not interested in you."

"Is that why she has been spending so much time with Vandoline? Is that the person responsible for my misery? I should have known." Pete was furious.

"There you go. It wasn't such a hard puzzle to build" Loveline said, relieved not having to name names.

"It is not true. Loveline, I think you and I have been too involved with each other. Now you are imagining things in order to justify our behavior? I have got to talk to Vandoline's husband" Pete said, refusing to accept what seemed obvious.

"Suit yourself. I just gave you the facts." Loveline fired back sarcastically.

"Pete came to me and learned more about Eve than he bargained for; the same painful story I am about to tell you"

Bruno continued, seeing how eager Albert was to hear the rest of his story.

"During Vandoline's visit to Cameroon we had an afternoon outing planned. Eve and I arrived at Vandoline's home at about the same time. Since we had some time to spare, we all sat in the living room and played games. But Eve and Vandoline kept glancing at each other and soon retired into Vandoline's room. This was followed by persistent intermittent giggling punctuated by uncharacteristic noises. I thought they were putting on make-up or doing female stuff.

Out of curiosity, I took a peek through a slit in the door" Bruno paused, looked around for tissue and blew his nose.

He got very emotional narrating the story. He hesitated, shook his head while looking down at the floor. The next part of the story brought him much discomfort but he had to let it out.

"They were doing female stuff quite alright" Bruno continued with a shaky voice. "They were kissing and touching each other in private places. Between them lay a huge artificial mushroom with two bean-shaped attachments at the base. It appeared wet, as if it had been dropped in water or dipped into something moist. Then Vandoline touched the mushroom with a familiar movement of the palm that caused me to look away."

"Are you confirming that they are, I mean were lesbians? No, that is not true!" Albert exclaimed and held his mouth wide open in surprise.

"Yes they are. They still are" Bruno said.

"Is that what she learned in America when she came to live here? Oh, such beautiful women, denying men the pleasure of their company. This is western contamination of our values, our people" Albert said.

"I will not blame it on the West, nor will I blame it on civilization. The Bible contains passages about homosexuality both in the old and the new testaments. That suggests to me it has been around since the creation of man and apparently transcends race and ethnicity. Civilization, freedom of expression and legalization has made it more prominent in some countries than in others. Even in countries, like Cameroon, where it is illegal, the very custodians of the law and top government officials are said to engage in homosexuality with their leaders in order to gain ministerial posts and/or maintain themselves in power. I believe there are homosexuals in Cameroon who have never been to America, nor have any connection to the West."

Bruno paused and looked at Albert who seemed confused and unsure what to say. "I guess I am not making any sense to you; I am not sure I understand what I am saying either. The pain of losing Vandoline is still very fresh, I guess. By the way, she had been leaning that way since high school. The occasional comments and actions did not make sense to me then but now I understand. Bottom line, it is not her coming to America that transformed her."

"Sorry, let's get back to the story. What did you do after you caught them in the act?" Albert asked.

"I went back to my seat and pretended I had seen nothing. They stayed in the room for at least 10 minutes. After that, we went out for lunch and stayed out till late in the night. However, what I had witnessed bothered me all night. Somehow, I convinced myself that my girlfriend getting intimate with another female was forgivable. I told myself I would have acted differently had she done it with another man. But was there really a difference? I believe the same, if not stronger, emotions and chemistry were involved in their act.

In any case, I began to understand why Eve was so controlling and interfering in the relationship between Vandoline and I. To Eve, I was just a dispensable boy toy, a smoke screen and, sometimes, an interference. It was clearly not their first time, it was the first time they had the audacity to do it while I was sitting a few feet away."

"But you should have said something, to someone, anyone" Albert went on.

"No way. As you already know, homosexuality is illegal in Cameroon. As is the case with many laws in Cameroon, the powerful are immune but the ordinary are not. I did not want

Vandoline and Eve to get into trouble with the law" Bruno rambled on.

"But you went ahead and married her. Or rather, I should be asking why she got married to a man" Albert said.

"I think she got married to meet the expectations of her parents and our society. The traditional Cameroonian expects every woman to get married to a man and have children. Vandoline was getting tired of her parents' persistent request for her to give them grandchildren before they died" Bruno explained.

"I understand the pressure from parents and society. What about you, why did you go along with it?" Albert pressed on.

"You know how badly we all wanted to come to America. She was my ticket to America. Besides, she had elevated me in society because I was nobody on my own, but as her fiancé, I had become a different person" Bruno said. "I also naively convinced myself that once we left Eve behind and came to the US, we would be happy together and whatever had transpired between them would be forgotten."

"Then Eve came here" Albert said leaning forward in his seat.

"Yes that is it. They started spending a lot of time together. I could have pretended they were just catching up on old times, but there was no lying what was going on. Eve was almost running my household, instructing my wife to tell me when to go and when to come. I was almost turned into a maid, running errands for both Vandoline and Eve. But I persevered until one evening, on my return from work, events took an unbearable turn"

"Hello honey, I am home. How was your day?" Bruno asked his wife on his return from work.

"Sorry, are you talking to me?" was her response.

"Yes I am talking to my wife. I don't have another honey, do I?" Bruno replied approaching her for a hug or a kiss.

"Honey my ass. See when you are returning from work. When are you going to make dinner for us and clean that mess in the kitchen?" she retorted.

"But honey, you have been here almost all day? You could have cleaned the kitchen or even started making dinner" Bruno said.

"Don't you honey me again. By the way, I am not your maid" she replied.

"You are not my maid neither am I yours. We are a couple and couples help each other" Bruno said.

"Look here, I saved your sorry ass from the hardship in your poor country. You might as well be my maid, show me some respect and appreciation. Get busy and make us something to eat" she pounced.

Bruno shook his head in disbelief as he headed to the kitchen. After a couple of hours, dinner was ready. Bruno had prepared Vandoline's favorite dish or so he thought.

"Honey food is ready. Come serve yourself" Bruno announced.

"I will eat right here, in front of the TV. My favorite show is on; I can't afford to miss any second of this show. I will have a cup of tea with my food" Vandoline replied.

"There is a commercial break. In those two minutes you can serve yourself. I will make the tea for you" Bruno replied.

Vandoline went ballistics. "How hard is it to put food on a plate, place it on a tray and walk the short distance from that kitchen to this living room? If you are going to live in this house you better show some responsibility. Bring me the food before I change my mind about eating."

Bruno served her food as requested.

"What is this? You call this dinner; this indigestible wild grass in a sea of oil? I don't need roughage and cholesterol, I need food" Vandoline said.

Bruno was shocked, first at the rage and, secondly, at her remarks about the food. She had always enjoyed that particular dish and had even cooked it not long ago.

"My dear, this was meant to be a treat, something to cheer you up. I know you love this food" Bruno said.

"Take it away; I can make my own food, okay."

"That is exactly what I had hoped. To come back to a delicious meal my wife had made. Instead what do I come back to? Aggression, aggression and more aggression. My walking through that door is all it takes to offend you these days" Bruno said.

"That is it. I am going to bed. By the way, you are sleeping on the couch again. And I am being considerate. You should be on the balcony or literally, in the dog house. Your snoring from the couch still keeps me awake in the bedroom" Vandoline lashed out as she stormed into the bedroom.

Bruno followed her to the bedroom. "What has happened to you, why are you so hard on me?" Bruno asked. After a short pause he added. "Never mind, I think I know but I love you so much I have chosen to stay blind."

"What do you mean? What do you know? That you can't satisfy me? That you are not man enough?" Vandoline kept pushing.

"That is exactly the point. I cannot satisfy you, no man can satisfy you. It is not about me. I know. I knew before we got married, I have known all along" Bruno said.

Bruno told her everything. He was hoping to see some remorse, perhaps an apology. Instead this triggered hostility. She was probably on drugs or something. Either that or she was drunken by the desire to be her real self, to stop living a double life.

She provoked Bruno into a fight and called the police to report domestic abuse. The self-inflicted bruise on her face served as evidence and Bruno was arrested and charged. In such situations in the USA, it is the woman's word against the man's.

Vandoline filed for divorce soon afterwards, and when Bruno attempted to resist, she promised to drop the domestic abuse charge in exchange for his cooperation. He decided he would rather settle for a divorce than have a criminal record. In the USA, divorce was the norm rather than the exception. Divorce could not prevent him from getting a job but a criminal conviction could.

After hearing Bruno's distressful story, Pete went back to apologize to Loveline. "Many things make sense to me now. All the time they spent together when Vandoline came to visit Cameroon. This set up started years ago, you know. Vandoline brought Eve and I together. She knew I was going to fall for her and marry her. Why was I so blind? This explains why Eve was more comfortable sleeping on another female's laps or bump and not on mine; and strange things like wanting to see other women naked. I dismissed it as some legacy from an all-girls boarding school."

"What are you going to do? There are definitely women out there who want you for who you are and are not using you as a ticket to a land where they can freely express themselves." Loveline said, finally betraying a hidden desire. She had become fond of Pete and saw a possibility of him leaving Eve for her.

"I can't give her that satisfaction of letting her go. She is stuck with me. I am as frustrated as she is but she will not get that freedom. She will have to continue doing it as an infidel" Pete insisted.

"You will have two infidels sharing the same bed, pretending to be married. How long will you keep that up? And what about me? Don't for one second think I will continue to be your booty call while you hang on to a hopeless marriage." Loveline said.

"It is obvious my marriage will not last. I will eventually let her go but I will not immediately get into another marriage after that. Loveline, you are my friend and we can remain that way, friends with some......you know what. It will be a while before I can give another woman any deep trust. I really appreciate your friendship but if you decide to move on, I will understand" Pete said.

Unlike Bruno, Pete is bent on turning the tables and frustrating Eve and Vandoline for as long as he can. He is succeeding but for how long will this last. This has the ingredients of a potential disaster that could cost lives. In the meantime Vandoline and Eve are enjoying "freedom" as best as they can.

"That, my friend, is my American dream. I had to forgo my university education in Cameroon to come here. How I wish I had completed my degree, I would have been more competitive on the job market. The American dream is still just a dream, my friend. Just a dream" Bruno concluded.

Albert opened his mouth to talk but could not find the words to use.

"I...but...I am sorry to hear this, my friend. I believe there are better days ahead."

6

Paul, the Powerful

Paul was next to visit Albert. He was happy to see Albert and especially pleased that Albert had finally made it to America. He claimed America was the place to be, but immediately contradicted himself with what he said next.

"Everyone has to work very hard here just to make ends meet. We do not have the luxury of strolling into work late in the morning, taking extended lunch breaks and leaving work early as was the case in the motherland" Paul said.

Paul was reminiscing on his work days back in Cameroon. How he used to go out for extended lunch breaks while patrons waited in line outside his office for his services. These were, by his standards, the good old days when each document for his signature had an unofficial fee. This bribe money was used for beer and multiple mistresses.

Paul was so corrupt he saw everything in life through a corrupt lens. He was a graduate of the lone school of public administration in Cameroon; a school that probably had a course on how to excel at corruption. Elections rigging 101 and strategies for hanging onto power 102 were compulsory courses in the curriculum. Loyalty to the national government and respect for France, the king maker, were also obligatory.

Paul had some qualities that amazed his professors and mates even in this school with a reputation for churning out corrupt graduates. He was the treasurer of the student union in his second year at the school. Just before the annual student gala, he withdrew a large sum of money for purchases and equipment rentals. Instead of paying for these things, he decided to take a trip to Bamenda, claiming there was a family emergency that required his presence. He returned to Yaounde without the money he had withdrawn.

When quizzed about the money he claimed he was in an accident on the way back and lost the money in the process. It was something from a former minister's play book. This minister once stunned the country with a proclamation that he left money floating in the air between Cameroon and France. The minister had apparently invented a money jet complete with a money pilot and money flight attendants, clearly giving life to money instead of using money to give a better life to people. This stunt had impressed his boss so much the minister had been promoted instead of being punished for leaving so much state money in flight.

Paul said he had spent a night in the hospital to recuperate from some internal injuries and a dislocated shoulder. Students and staff believed him and showed a lot of sympathy, only to discover one week later that he had not been in any accident. There had been an accident but he had not been in that vehicle or anywhere near it.

Weeks later Paul wrote a motion of support for himself and his president, made his friend sign and sent it to the students' union. Paul's action was a small scale display of a bigger problem, like the government drafting its own motion of support before changing the constitution to make Lionman president for life, like corrupt ministers faking a motion of support from their constituents to give the president an illusion of popularity in one region of the country more than the other.

Paul agreed to pay back the union money he had spent and borrowed this money from a friend. Paul had counterfeit foreign currency that he had tried to convert into local currency without luck. When time came to pay his friend, he chose to give him this counterfeit money. His friend went to convert this in a bank and was almost arrested. When he confronted Paul about it, Paul opted for aggressive tactics.

"Have you forgotten who you are talking to? I am in the school of administration and my father is a retired police officer. Do you know I can get you arrested with just a simple phone call?" Paul threatened his friend.

"Is this how I get paid for my kindness; with threats and violence? Where was your retired police officer dad when you needed money? By the way, being a police officer's son should have taught you some morals. You should have learned from him that counterfeiting, cheating and stealing are crimes. Oh what am I saying? He was one of those thieves collecting bribes from drivers and conniving with armed robbers to steal from ordinary citizens. He has trained you well, like father like son, I should say. Get me arrested if you want, God will pay you back for this injustice. You may never find peace in this world if you don't pay me back and apologize for this act" his friend lashed out.

"We never apologize to ordinary people. I am now in the big leagues, my friend" Paul concluded with finality and walked away. Another useful quality for anyone who would be in Lionman's government; threaten and bully any opposition even when there is a legitimate claim. Silence any voice that seeks to reveal your corrupt nature.

During one of his exams Paul had cheat sheets stuffed in his socks. The professor noticed him going under his desk a couple of times. When Paul saw the professor looking, he pretended to have itchy feet.

"These jiggers will not let me concentrate on my exams. I shouldn't have gone to the village last week" he whispered to the professor when he came to take a closer look. His neighbors got a good laugh from this lame excuse.

The professor eventually snuck on Paul from behind and noticed papers sticking out of his socks.

"Give me all those papers you have in your socks" the professor ordered Paul.

"What papers sir?" he asked, looking surprised.

"Don't play dumb with me. Pull out all those papers from your socks and give me" the professor insisted.

"There are no papers in my socks sir. This is the nature of my socks sir. They are designer socks sir, made puffy on the sides to protect the ankle sir" Paul babbled.

Since cheating and rigging elections was a job description for these folks, it was logical to expect these skills being put to practice in the school. Paul's argument could be rephrased thus "I did not switch the ballot box; the box came with the deciding votes and I see nothing wrong with that."

Some students sailed through the school without ever sitting for an exam. Any professors who attempted to hold back these privileged students found themselves at the receiving end of threats from influential government officials and ministers.

As in everything else, the underprivileged poor students got the occasional harsh punishment if caught cheating, which meant they had to find more bribe money for a mediator to plead with the professor or negotiate with a school administrator. Talk about a vicious cycle of bribery and corruption. Students bribe to get in, bribe to stay in, bribe to graduate and bribe to be appointed to a duty post with a big budget. Once at the post they start stealing money and collecting bribes to pay back what was spent to get in. Of course, this becomes an addiction and they only keep raising the bar higher and higher.

Upon graduation, Paul was made the sub divisional officer of a rural municipality. That made him the most powerful man in the sub division and also gave him an opportunity to make money. Conflicts between villages were settled in favor of the highest bidder. The rich always won the land dispute cases, cattle breeders who gave him the fat bulls could chase out the crop farmers from their fields and political opponents were arrested and only released after healthy bribes were paid.

Paul also enjoyed official visits to villages under his jurisdiction. The official business was hardly the highlight of these visits; it was the unwritten entertainment code for every visiting top government or elected official. The most beautiful, sometimes under aged, female in the village was sent to his room as personal entertainment. Other males in his entourage also got this privilege.

Ironically, he was part of delegations promoting the fight against HIV/AIDS. Slogans like one man one woman; abstinence will not kill you; protect yourself and your partner, use condoms were usually part of the message. Paul taught this message during the day and did the opposite at night or at lunch breaks. He was the do-what-I-say and not what-I-do kind of preacher.

Fortunately, he never contracted HIV. Had he been HIV positive, he would have been an effective vehicle for spreading this virus across his jurisdiction.

His colleague in another municipality had died of AIDS, and shortly thereafter, there had been a string of AIDS related illnesses and deaths in the villages. This had started with his sex partners and had spread to their partners or spouses. Everyone knew he had spread the virus around and he had been nicknamed "Friendly Bio-gun" after he had continued having unprotected sex following the HIV diagnosis. His organ was considered a bio-gun and his tadpoles were bio-bullets spiked with HIV. In some North American countries, men like him were tried and jailed, a good way of stopping his evil intentions. Sadly, if such persons became big financial burdens, this country sent them back to their place of origin to go spread their load to their own with reckless abandon; like deploying friendly biological bombs to poor countries.

As long as Paul stayed loyal to the ruling party, his superiors ignored his excesses. However, he eventually did the unpardonable by openly supporting an opposition party. He had been promised a ministerial position if the opposition came to power. Greed had caused him to fall very hard for this. He imagined how much more he could make as a minister and in charge of huge contracts. He imagined 10% of these multimillion contracts going straight into his bank account. He imagined the bogus field trips and the associated per diems. He envisioned having mistresses of a different category, probably supermodels, top musicians, the most beautiful journalists and possibly other ministers. He dreamt of mansions abroad, shares in western companies and expensive vacations to some tropical paradise outside Africa.

Paul's super boss, the senile lion at the top of the shaky pyramid, had a slogan: never bite the hand that feeds you. Unfortunately Paul had done just that.

He was dismissed and arrested shortly afterwards. He found himself in the same jail he had sent many people to. Consequently, he endured torture from the prison guards and torment from the persons he had thrown in jail.

"Mr. Paul, you put me here. I told you that God will pay you back for the injustice I suffered in your hands. Today you are facing the music and I am happy to see you here" one of the farmers he had sent to jail told him.

"I don't remember you. What did I do to you?" Paul asked.

"I am not surprised you have forgotten me. I have been here in this hell hole called 'awaiting trial' for years. I have still not had my day in court and I will probably never have it because there is no one out there looking out for me. Putting me here was a life sentence and I hope you get the same thing, that is, if one of the other guys you put here doesn't kill you soon" the farmer said.

The other detainees decided humiliation was the best revenge for Paul. First he had to pay what prisoners called 'new man tax', a levy that every new detainee had to pay to the person who had been in prison the longest. His amount was ten times the usual levy.

"I am being lenient with you Mr. Paul. You know your father put me here, right? He framed me because we were dating the same woman. He was married to your mother at the time and I was a bachelor. I have been here for over fifteen years awaiting trial and destiny has brought you to me. This might just be my opportunity for revenge but I am in no rush. We will take it slowly. Let me have your 'new man tax' fast else I will start torturing you right now" the senior prisoner, Grand Alfredo, said with a deep voice that terrified Paul.

"I am sorry for what my father did to you" Paul said with a shaky voice that betrayed his fear.

"Look at him. You are already shaking when we have not done anything to you yet. Don't be sorry for what your father did, be sorry for the trouble you caused all these guys" Grand Alfredo pointed at men sitting around him, staring at Paul with blood shot eyes. "Give me the money."

"I did not know about this tax sir. I will arrange for some money to be brought in tomorrow please" Paul pleaded.

"You can call your father to bring in some money. The phone call will cost you the same amount as your tax. I am pretty sure you can afford it." Grand Alfredo handed him a cell phone. Cell phones were not allowed in prison but Grand Alfredo had come to an arrangement with the guards and had a cell phone in there for a long time.

Paul made the call and his father quickly brought money he needed.

"We will let you sleep tonight but you will be on toilet duty tomorrow" Grand Alfredo told Paul, after receiving his tax money.

His sleeping space was a bare floor at the corner of the jail, next to the bowls that served as toilets. The stench, coupled with fear for his life kept him fully awake all night.

"Good morning big man. I hope you slept well" Grand Alfredo asked, slapping Paul hard on the back. Paul let out a loud cry to the amusement of everyone in the room. "You are not man enough now? I thought you were the most powerful man in your area. One night in prison has turned you into a baby? Better toughen up or you will die soon. It doesn't mean that I care anyway, but I want you to suffer for as long as I have."

The second night Paul was convinced of his eminent death and wanted out of jail at all cost. He devised a plan and this included Grand Alfredo. He was going to use Grand Alfredo's phone during the day to talk to his father. He promised Grand Alfredo a tempting sum of money in exchange for the phone call. It was an offer Grand Alfredo could not turn down. It was enough money to bribe the guards numerous times for sneak outs into town at night.

It was common for prisoners to bribe their way out of detention for a few hours. Why they always returned remains a mystery. The guards were even rumored to occasionally release seasoned criminals at night to go rob homes and people. They usually got part of the loot, especially cash.

Paul called his father and asked him to perform an act for which he was usually at the receiving end; bribe the guards to let him out. But this was a big ask for a political prisoner like Paul. Anyone who freed this class of prisoners stood the risk of becoming a prisoner himself.

Paul's father, Clinton Mamba, went to work immediately, starting his negotiations with the guards on duty.

"My son has been threatened with death by his cell mates. I need to get him out of here soon. What can I do to make it possible?" Clinton asked the supervising guard.

"Inspector" the guard used Clinton's police title. Titles are very important to Cameroonians. People wear their titles on their foreheads and once someone gets a title it is his for life, even after he retires. "I am not surprised that those guys want to kill your son. He put most of them in there" the guard said, with no sympathy.

"Unfortunately, he cannot be released after what he has done to the government that gave him so much power, power that he used to oppress all of us around here. Guess what, it gave me pleasure to give him some lashes this morning."

"Please help me release my son. Name your price; I will get it for you. I know what happens to prisoners like him and I don't want to bury my son, I want him to bury me" Clinton begged.

"Inspector, I know you can afford any amount of bribe we ask. After all, you and your son amassed a lot of wealth in that way. But I can't help you. This one is beyond our powers. If you like you can go talk to our director" the guard said.

"I understand. I will go to your director but there is something you can do for me. Please, threaten the other prisoners with severe punishment if they maltreat my son" Clinton said and handed the guard an envelope.

"Thank you. We will try our best. Good luck with the director" the guard said, pleased with the content of the envelope.

Another night came and, as if sleeping by the toilet bowl wasn't bad enough, water was poured on Paul's sleeping spot. In the morning he lay motionless while his cell mates rushed for breakfast. Grand Alfredo kicked him on the side but he did not move. The guards were alerted and Paul taken to the main office. In the office he started shaking like a leaf in a storm and his teeth clattering like a stack of plates on a Camrail train. All he could say was "malaria sir….hospital please."

He was taken to the hospital. Treatment for malaria, which included intravenous infusion of physiological saline containing antimalarial drugs, was initiated immediately. No blood test was done to confirm that he indeed had malaria.

Paul's father came to see him at the hospital. Once he was alone with his father, he told him where his money was hidden and arranged for the money and his passport to be brought to the hospital. It was common place for government officials to have suitcases full of money in their homes.

Night came and Paul's father worked with nurses to distract the guard on duty outside his hospital ward. This comprised offering the guard a generous amount of whisky in small sachets, which he voraciously sucked. One of the sachets was infused with a sleeping pill which helped knock him out. Had he respected the code of conduct not to drink alcohol while on duty, he would have avoided this trap.

With the guard unconscious, a window of opportunity was created…an open window for Paul to escape through.

Paul had not actually been sick. He had just pulled one of his many stunts which left people wondering what he was going to do next. If the occasion ever arose, he would possibly fake his own death.

Paul traveled all night into a neighboring country and from there to the USA, in a style very similar to Pa Mola's escape from Cameroon.

In America, Paul has to actually work for a living, not just live off his title and position. However, old habits hardly go away. Paul is a cashier at a local store. He has been a cashier for a very long time. Many employees have come after him and have been promoted to senior positions, but Paul's attitude is holding him back. Less than a month into this job, he had wanted to be promoted. He bragged that he was trained to be a leader and he would become the store manager in the near future. It was a worthy dream but his work ethic did not match that dream. He still hung on to that spirit of entitlement characteristic of his training and job in his motherland. He was also still lacking honesty in very trivial things.

As a cashier, he was required to advertise the store credit cards and get customers to obtain them. He was forceful in his pursuit of customers in this regard. Those who were cautious about their credit standing would refuse but he did not take no for an answer. That in itself could be a good business quality, if boundaries are respected. Some customers yielded to his pressure tactics and filled the applications. When an application was rejected because of bad credit, he would lie to the customer.

"Your request is pending a response. The credit card company will send you information after a couple of days."

Once the customers left, he would turn to his colleagues and crack jokes about their poor credit and how it would even get worse with another inquiry. He would be too oblivious of the disgust on the faces around him. No qualities of a potential manager.

It is beginning to dawn on him that he might never become manager, not in this store, not in any store. His second job as a late night cab driver is becoming more difficult. He recently slept behind the wheel briefly because of fatigue and that frightened him.

He now wishes for a single stable job with regular hours that pays well. Consequently, he has decided to train for something else, something that will put him on the fast track to become the head where ever he finds himself. He is not sure what that will be; business administration is a good possibility.

How I wish I had stayed loyal to Lionman's regime, he often thinks regretfully. *I would probably be a governor by now. Oh greed, look where you have led me; from the seat of power, freebies and respect (or better still, fear), to this; this life where I am barely noticed.*

Despite all the challenges, Paul considers himself lucky to be a free man. He knows he does not deserve asylum in the USA.

7

Matt the cheat

"I am glad to see you my friend. Welcome man" Matt said as he grabbed Albert's hand and gave him a shoulder to shoulder bump.

"Thank you. How have you been?" Albert asked.

"So so. Man, in this place, you have to hustle. It is a tough life. Nothing is free here" Matt said

"But nothing is free anywhere. You have to work for everything" Albert said.

"You are right. That is why I run my business during the day and moonlight as a security officer. No time to relax, no time to have fun" Matt said.

Matt was a business man in Cameroon before leaving for the USA. He supplied building material for construction projects in villages and small towns. His clients were government and private contractors. He usually received 50% advance pay and the rest when he supplied the products.

At some point, he had collected a large amount of money from his customers. He had convinced some to pay him the full amount upfront. Unbeknownst to these customers, Matt had secured a visa to attend his sister's wedding in the USA. He quietly left the country behind desperate customers with unfinished projects. Some contractors were jailed by their powerful clients for failing to deliver on their contracts. Poor villagers were left with uncompleted buildings.

Matt stayed in the USA after his sister's wedding. He put together a strong case for asylum, claiming he was being hunted in his country for his political views. He had been preparing for this day by writing articles and commentaries against the ruling party in some local newspapers. He had kept clippings of these articles. A letter from the newspaper editor, whom he had paid, supported Matt's claims.

Matt was right about one thing, he would have been arrested had he returned to Cameroon; not for his political views, but for his corrupt business practices. After ripping off his clients, he had received angry and threatening emails which helped bolster his asylum case. He had distorted the facts saying the claims from his customers were just a smear campaign by agents of the government. He was granted asylum.

Matt had started a business in the USA, selling used computers and refurbished cell phones. His clients were mainly visitors and students from other African countries. His best clients were those returning to their home country with no hope of coming back to the USA. To these clients, he would sell faulty cell phones and computers that were certain to stop working after a few hours of use. If any client returned and complained, he would refuse to replace the product and would make them look stupid in addition. A fast talker full of empty rhetoric, he usually fatigued his customers into submission. Consumer protection took no action against him despite numerous complaints from his clients. It was the: they are doing it to themselves so just let them be, kind of reaction.

In his night job, Matt spent all working hours sleeping. He was more of an insecurity than a security guard. He knew when his supervisors did their rounds and set his alarm to be awake at those times. When he could not sleep, he went around looking in dumpsters for abandoned electronics that could be sold to unfortunate clients.

Matt recently decided it was time to get a wife and arranged for his family to get him a beautiful young woman from Cameroon. He is saving money and preparing documents to send for her to come to America. He proudly carries her picture with him everywhere.

"Hey did you see my wife to be? Look at this picture, isn't she beautiful?" Matt asked Albert.

"Oh yes she is and she is very young too" Albert said.

"Of course, she has to be young. *Eheh, na young blood I want, you know me*" Matt bragged in pidgin. "She thinks she is getting married to an engineer. That is what I told my parents to tell her. I have heard she brags about me to her friends. She tells them that I am this great electrical engineer or whatever, that I make computers and other electronics and can also repair any electronic device on planet earth."

"Come on Matt, why do you have to lie to her? If you are serious about marrying this woman, you should tell her the truth" Albert advised.

"But I am not far from the truth. I sell electronics, I clean them very well when I pick them from the dump and I can even rescue some of them. America has devised big names for casual jobs and trades so I might as well magnify my own. You know what else, I am not a night watchman, I am a security guard. It is more dignifying and politically correct" Matt tried to justify his lies.

"You know the truth and it is up to you to tell it now and prevent future troubles. I can understand why these women disappear once they get here. They get here and discover the liar they got married to and that leaves them no other choice but to run away" Albert said.

Matt pondered the point for a moment and agreed.

"You might be right. I have a colleague at my security job also from Africa. He lied to his would be wife that he was an engineer but his actual job at the time was at a poultry abattoir. His friends dubbed him the de-feathering engineer. He married the woman and brought her to America but the marriage did not last more than six months because his wife discovered his lies about his job and other things. She said she would have stayed with him had he told her the truth."

"You should learn from your colleague's mistake and do things differently" Albert said, delighted Matt was coming to his senses.

"Hey, I am smoother than that guy. My woman will not understand the difference and even if she does, I will sweet talk her into forgiving and forgetting. Look at me, which woman can be angry with this handsome guy."

Albert was disappointed but gave up trying to convince Matt. He was exhibiting a toxic mixture of behavioral defects. If pride goes before the downfall of a man, the mixture of pride, arrogance and stupidity can only spell calamities.

"I can't wait to get my woman out of that corrupt country" Matt continued. "Man, you see, we are here suffering like this because of the corruption in our country. Look at our ministers; they have huge bank accounts abroad. Money from our oil exports goes into private accounts. State property is used as if it were private property. And did you know the head of state can just request for cash from banks and businesses as if he owned them? It all reminds me of the mafia, you either pay the mafia boss some protection money or loss your business. That is our country and that is why I am here. Sad isn't it?" Matt rambled.

Albert got exasperated when Matt started this rambling about corruption in Cameroon. This was an opportunity to confront his friend. He had been appalled when Matt had dealt his customers in Cameroon a dirty blow before departing the country.

"It is true that our government is corrupt. It is true that most people in the Diaspora would be back there if the money hidden in bank accounts overseas was not stolen from the people at all; or had been invested in the country by these thieves to create employment locally instead of making the rich western banks even richer. They lie, steal and cheat, but yet are called honorable ministers or members of parliament. I guess the honor in this case is as in honor killing, where members of some hard core religions kill women for going against their religious beliefs. There is nothing honorable in this kind of killing, just like there is nothing honorable in ministers depriving the youths of a descent future, killing their country and sometimes killing these youths for protesting. And the president - Lionman - is still referred to as His Excellency (H.E.). If we assume this means excellence for country, then the title is oxymoronic for president Lionman. The only things he excels at are destroying his country (or personal estate as it seems), absenteeism, misuse of state property, stealing state funds, political vendetta and most especially, defending interests of his French master at the detriment of his own people. Perhaps he should be H.E.C.K. (His Exceedingly Corrupt King) instead of H.E. Lionman. We have to speak out and do something against these acts of corruption as much as we can" Albert said.

"This thirst for power, selfishness and excessive corruption is so imbibed into the system I often wonder what it will take to break this hyper-vicious cycle. It may sound naïve but Cameroon has gotten to a point that only a spiritual revolution can purge the system. A revolution like we saw in Nigeria in the 1990s when Christians stood together in one voice for a change in their country, national leadership included. They were convinced that, as the Bible says, the prayer of righteous men could release tremendous power.

They also believed Matthew 18:19 that if they were in agreement on whatever they asked, God will do it for them. However, if agreement is key in this matter, then Cameroon still has a long way to go. A church that canonizes corrupt and cultic leadership cannot be in agreement with the Holy Spirit and it is this Holy Spirit that puts all Christians on the same page. A politicized and polarized church cannot pray for the carpet to be pulled from under its feet. That said, we serve a God of miracles and it is not too late for righteous leaders to rise up and pray for change" Albert continued in this outburst that demonstrated his anger with the government and its cultic leader.

Matt looked pleased that they finally agreed on at least one thing.

"But why is it that we see corruption only as a government affair?" Albert continued. "When we take money from people, fail to provide the goods they paid for and run out of the country, that is corruption; when we defraud fellow immigrants with faulty products, that is corruption.

Our third world government is the place where corruption and greed meet opportunity, and then every corrupt act is ramped up. At the end of the day, our complaint is not about the ministers being corrupt; our frustration is that we are not given an equal opportunity to steal; that we are not given our fair share of the national cake. You know, the Bible says he who is not faithful with small things cannot be trusted with big ones" Albert went on, with a passion that surprised Matt.

"Are you saying we are all corrupt? Are you calling me corrupt? Because if you are I can tell you right now that….."

Albert interrupted Matt before he could complete his sentence or threat.

"Yes, we are all corrupt or facilitators in one way or the other. We quickly give out that bribe for our document to be signed; we agree to sacrifice half of our accrued salaries in order for the other half to be paid; we give back 10% of our contracts to the minister or whoever in government is in charge, then do a bad job and bribe the inspectors to certify the project as complete; we refuse to pay tax on our businesses and rather bribe the tax collector with a fraction of what we owe; we bribe to get into law enforcement and get our bribe back by collecting money from criminals and drivers; we get paid a full salary but put in half the hours of work and the list can go on and on. Where is the government in all of these?" Albert asked.

"Okay, Mr. Morality. I have heard enough of your preaching. You are now in America, let's see you get asylum without compromising your moral standards or whatever you call it" Matt said, visibly upset but also a little pensive. Albert had apparently struck a nerve.

"I can choose to go back home. I did not soil my hands before leaving the country. You know the African proverb: if you defecate at the door on your way out of the house, you will have to clean the poop before getting back in? You left a big one, I left nothing" Albert pushed back.

"*Dey send you for ma back?*" Matt asked in pidgin as he departed. "*Stay with your malchance, I don go.*"

Albert did not see or hear from Matt after this.

8

What about a success story?

"Life seems hard for most of our friends here in the USA. What is going on? Is it that hard to live here?" Albert asked Samson.

"Yes, it is tough for most people. In this country, the average person is one pay cheque away from homelessness. To be honest, it is a hand to mouth life for most people from university professors to postdoctoral fellows to the store employee or the custodian" Samson replied.

"No, it is not really a hand to mouth as such. That will be even better. The reality is people live on credit; buy today and pay tomorrow. The day you can't pay, you loss everything, file for bankruptcy and lose the ability to borrow in the future. It is complicated" Samson continued.

"Back home, we think everybody in the US is doing great. They come home every Christmas and show off, spending large sums of money, wearing expensive clothes and driving big cars. We are left with the impression that life is very easy; that they make a lot of money" Albert said.

"Some people do. Doctors, pharmacists, nurses, lawyers and other professionals may make a lot of money. These people can afford to travel to Cameroon or anywhere and live comfortably with relative ease. These are few amongst Cameroonians. The majority of those who go home and show off actually have to do more than two jobs to save enough money for traveling. As for the expensive outfits, some use credit cards to purchase them. They make sure the price tags are left intact. Once back here, these items are returned to the shops for a refund" Samson explained.

"That explains a situation I witnessed in Cameroon. A young man got into a brawl in a bar while visiting Cameroon. He suffered a cut and his suit was stained with blood. He was losing a lot of blood but seemed less concerned about that. He complained about the ruined suit and how much money it was going to cost him if it got ruined. He had withstood a beating without crying. Tough guy, we thought. But when he discovered the suit had been badly ripped, he let out a loud cry; a thousand dollar cry, for that was the cost of the suit. A blood stain could be salvaged with detergents, but a ripped suit was a dead end. Now I understand. That was a thousand dollars on his credit card, to be paid for by months of hard labor" Albert narrated.

"That is what I am talking about" Samson said.

"But the false impression that life is easy for everyone here encourages people like me to abandon their jobs and come here to join the bandwagon. If we could just get the real picture, people would make more informed choices" Albert lamented.

"I agree. However, most people prefer to hear the lie. The truth is perceived as selfishness. They think we want to keep them away from an easy life; a life of abundance; like the biblical Promised Land flowing with milk and honey, they imagine.

For some people, however, coming to America is the only way to lead a half descent life. For instance, the jobless university graduates who have resorted to selling cigarettes on small trays at bus stops and many other people who are completely helpless in Cameroon. For these categories, an opportunity to leave the country will be taken no matter what you tell them. That is understandable. On the other hand, just like you have said, those with stable jobs need to know what they are getting into before leaving their jobs to come here" Samson said.

"Well, like you said, it is not all gloomy. There are some great success stories, like yours. You are a well-respected surgeon" Albert said.

"Thank you. I worked hard for it. There were days I regretted leaving a well-paid job in one of the best private hospitals in Cameroon to come and start all over again. I packed and unpacked several times, wanting to go back home. After a while, I decided I had to find a way forward right here" Samson said.

Samson came to the USA as a permanent resident thanks to the diversity visa program. Unfortunately, permanent residency did not guarantee him a job as a surgeon. He had to go through a long certification process to qualify as a surgeon.

In the meantime, Samson got a job as a custodian in a local hospital and a dish washer in a fast food restaurant. He worked hard during the day and studied hard at night.

What an irony. In Cameroon, he had his garbage emptied at the click of a finger. In America, the tables were turned. He was cleaning up after the doctors, nurses and interns. Occasionally, he would choose to empty the trash when interns were discussing the disease files. He almost gave in to the temptation to contribute an idea on one or two occasions.

He still had to take care of the financial commitments in Cameroon. He sent money to his parents and siblings in Cameroon from each pay cheque. Although his finances were stretched, he continued to support his parents and siblings while keeping aside some money to register for the medical board exams.

When time came to register for the exams, the first challenge was obtaining transcripts from his former university. It wasn't unusual for a request for transcripts to go unanswered for several months. Samson's dad had to make several trips to the university secretariat for the transcript to be released. Although the transcript was legitimate, someone in the office had to receive a gift on top of the official fees for the document to be released. And what did the request say? That the transcript be mailed directly to the given address! Who cared? You either got a relative or friend to collect and mail it for you or you waited till the cows came home. Samson's father ensured the document was mailed through a reliable courier.

Samson was required to pass the two step medical licensing examination. Many of his former colleagues had attempted this without success and had settled for physician assistants and other jobs unrelated to medicine such as cab drivers or security guards.

When Samson failed in his first attempt at the step one exam, his former colleagues and friends began to discourage him. In a paraphrase of the bible, they said it was easier for a camel to pass through a needle's eye than for an Africa trained physician to pass the medical board certification. He was encouraged to focus on other career options; else he would write exams the rest of his life.

At first, Samson listened to the negative comments and relented on his preparation for the exams. He considered going back to Cameroon, but despite the struggles, he had become used to some of the conveniences and luxuries that were available to almost everybody in the USA.

Does life have to be this way, Samson thought. *It imposes change on you, withholds the things you cherish and teases you enough with a combination of distractions to keep you from focusing on what is important. Focus, Samson, focus*, he concluded.

Samson went back to his books and prepared hard for the exams. The detractors however, did not give up.

Joe was most persistent at discouraging Samson. He was a failure in many ways and hated seeing others succeed where he had failed. He was known as "Dr Abort" even before he graduated from medical school. This was because he had set up an abortion clinic in his bedroom and performed numerous abortions while just three years into his medical training. His clients were high school and university students as well as prostitutes who failed to use condoms during intercourse.

As expected, his technique was crude and dangerous and most of his clients ended up with complications. Because they were usually too embarrassed to talk about it, these clients suffered in silence and took medicines obtained from road side vendors to alleviate their pains.

However, Joe's business would soon take a terrible turn. One of Joe's clients died shortly after he had performed his crude procedure on her. Before she died, she told her roommate what had happened. This information was relayed to her parents who reported the incident to the police. Joe was arrested and jailed. However, he was able to buy his way out of prison with money he had accumulated from his abortion business. His criminal record also disappeared in the process. A clean slate for Dr. Abort!

Joe went on to graduate from medical school and was the talk of the town. He wore the doctor title on his forehead. During a visit to his village, everyone he saw on the street received a diagnosis for diseases they probably didn't have. In violation of confidentiality laws and professional ethics, he broadcasted the status of all HIV positive patients in the village to everyone who cared to listen. Shortly after graduating Joe moved to the US and tried unsuccessfully to get licensed as a doctor.

Knowing this much about Joe, Samson decided to ignore him and other detractors and focus on getting his medical board certification.

"I do not want to be limited by the mental attitude of the people around me. Most importantly, I don't want my own thinking to pull me down. We have a tendency to think too small. Once we have a job outside our training we become contented with it and refuse to seek growth. We aim low and shoot even lower. I want to aim high, even if I shoot low, it will not be below the belt. My friend, we are in the land of dreams, and if we have chased it this far and decided to stay, why limit it, why not dream big, why accept the status quo? I chose to look at the success stories and draw inspiration from them, rather than focus on and identify with the failures. I chose the *'audacity of hope'* like Barack Obama" Samson told Joe.

In his second attempt, Samson passed the first step and went on to pass the next step. Luck continued to smile on him and he was granted an opportunity for residency in a university hospital.

As an immigrant, he faced a lot more challenges during his residency but stayed determined, keeping his eyes on the bigger picture. His fellow interns admired his knowledge of tropical diseases and learned a lot from him while he also learned more from them about the common American ailments such as diabetes, depression, cancer or obesity.

After a couple of years of hard work and a final exam, Samson got licensed and got a decent job thereafter. Then he sponsored his siblings and other relatives to study and live in the USA. They all lived in a comfortable environment, studied hard and have since become very successful in their careers.

9

To stay or not to stay

Albert had a decision to make, stay in America and build a case for asylum or return to Cameroon. Because he had left Cameroon during the long school vacation, he was not missing any work. He had also come a month ahead of his course and still had time to attend it.

Albert attended the course; the primary reason for which he had been given a visa. It was a very educative experience. The moderators emphasized the importance of returning home and training their colleagues and other professionals in the field.

However, Albert was still struggling with whether or not to go back to Cameroon. If he had to go, it had to be before the start of the school year. With a month to go before the start of the school year, he decided to make the best of his time while contemplating his future. He visited as many places as possible.

Whenever he had the chance to spend time with Samson, he made the best of it; seeking advice on key issues and asking him questions about his American experience.

"If you knew what you know now, would you have left Cameroon to come to the US?" Albert asked Samson.

"As you already know, I went through a rough time when I arrived. But my life has changed; I am as successful as any surgeon can be in this country. In that regard, I can categorically tell you that I would do it again if I had to start all over. However, ask other people that question and you will get completely different answers" Samson responded.

"I wish it were that easy for me to decide on staying. I wish there were a way of knowing the future; knowing whether I will be granted asylum, get a job in my field and have a successful career in America. I wish we had those villagers who throw down some cowries, hold your hand and read your future. Oh, wait a minute, they are no different from what the Americans call psychic readers. Maybe I should consult one" Albert lamented.

"I wish I could help you my friend. The decision to stay or go back is totally up to you. I can assure you the path will not be easy and what lies at the end of the tunnel usually is unpredictable; what looks like a light could be another challenge coming your way. If you succeed, you will say it was totally worth it but if you end up in perpetual despair, you will wish you had stayed in Cameroon. What is keeping many people here is their children; the American dream has escaped most first generations but they continue to see or hope for a future for their children. In some cases, these children are on the right path but in some cases, the disappointment has already gone beyond one generation" Samson said. "By the way, I assume you resigned from your job in Cameroon. Will they let you reclaim it if you go back?"

"Resigned? Nobody resigns from their job before leaving Cameroon. I know a colleague who had decided to leave his job the proper way; give a resignation letter in advance and hand in all school property in his possession. When he submitted his resignation letter, his school principal advised him to just walk away from the job. That way, he would continue receiving his salary for as long as possible. In exchange for this advice, he could give the principal postdated cheques for a fraction of the salary. The principal made every effort to convince my colleague it was a win win situation; that many had done it and never been caught" Albert narrated.

"In the USA, without the adequate advance notice, an employee is required to pay the employer; in Cameroon, it is a win win situation?" Samson asked.

"The principal was right that many had done it. In fact, my former colleagues currently in the USA are still receiving salaries from the Cameroonian Government years after leaving the country. Some professors, teachers, medical doctors and other former government employees who had since gained US citizenship are possibly still on the Cameroon Government payroll. Simply put, the Cameroon Government is probably giving naturalized Americans, possibly Canadians, British, Germans and French free money; directly into their now overseas (Cameroon) bank accounts. When there is a scheduled census of the civil service in Cameroon, these foreigners rush in, answer the roll call and hop on the next flight back to their new countries. And the same people blame their being in the Diaspora on corruption in their place of birth" Albert lamented.

"What did Stephen Covey say? We judge others by their actions and ourselves by our intentions" Samson said.

"Amongst you here in America are some very good people; highly respectable and trustworthy. Yet amongst you are some bad ones. Like Paul who borrowed good money from friends and chose to pay back with counterfeit money because his police connections will shield him and also went on to committed crimes against humanity, like Matt the cheat, like Pa Mola who stole money from the government in Cameroon and adopted a dead man's identity in the US. You also have murderers, sexual predators and people who committed other terrible crimes in Cameroon. They have all found refuge in this country. Apparently there is a code of silence amongst you; just don't report any of these criminals to law enforcement because you will look bad. I think those who stole from the government and tax payers should be sent back to face justice; those who committed crimes against humanity should be tried right here" Albert said.

"My friend, my mind is made up" Albert continued. "I will go back to Cameroon. I will miss luxuries like good roads, clean streets, steady electricity, uninterrupted water supply, high speed internet and the absolute freedom of speech and expression. However, I will not miss the vestiges of racism that still exist in some communities in this country" Albert said.

"I respect your decision my friend. You will probably not miss any of those things once you spend a few weeks in Cameroon. You might even have clean streets should a French president visit the country. Remember the last time one agreed to visit? Lionman went on the radio, television and all newspapers to announce that the master was coming. A large chunk of our national budget was dedicated towards planning for this visit. The streets were not only swept, they were scrubbed with detergent all the way from the airport to the Lion's den. The frontages of all houses along the streets were white washed, beggars and mentally deranged people were removed from streets and dumped in nearby villages or camps. These hungry beggars who could have been fed for a whole year with a fraction of the money spent on this august visit were better hidden, not to let the master know that we have such a problem in Cameroon of all places. The best French wines and champagnes were brought in. Like Francis Nyamnjoh said in *The Disillusioned African*, Cameroonians consume what they don't produce and produce what they don't consume. The example comes right from the top. Anyway, the French president arrived amidst all the fanfare and hypocrisy and probably did not notice the clean streets and the whitewashed buildings" Samson lamented.

"And you know the funniest thing? Lionman offered the French man French wine, showing the master how well assimilated he was. 'Look at me, I am almost like you, my master, I consume French. I hope you are impressed with me, the faithful caretaker of your backyard.' For some reason his French guest opted for a local beer, a slap in the face and probably a lesson for his puppet to promote his own products to foreign visitors" Albert added.

"By the way, let's come back to talking about you" Samson said. "Where did the notion of unlimited freedom in America come from? For some people, freedom is not knowing that your every conversation is being recorded, every move tracked and your life virtually an open book. The freedom in this case is simply ignorance; ignorance of the limits of that perceived freedom. But if you have nothing to hide you can't be bothered.

Freedom of expression has its limits too. If you are a demographically privileged talk show host, with a name like Brush Bug, you can wish the American president failure and go totally free. On the other hand, Ahmed can't say the same thing; he will be on the terrorist watch list, no fly list and all the blacklists you can imagine. He could even be charged with treason. So there is no absolute freedom. However, it is closer to absolute for some than for others" Samson told his friend.

"As for racism" Samson continued. "You are right. It still exists and has to be strongly condemned. There has been progress, significant progress I believe. However, racism minus the race factor is just another superiority complex. Superiority complex drives one group to look at another as inferior and thus treat it as such. This is the theory of relative superiority as aptly described by Nyamnjoh in *The Disillusioned African*. If we look at it that way, then most, if not all of us are guilty of discrimination against fellow mankind. That is why in Africa, one tribe goes out and destroys another and captures survivors as slaves, that is why we call some people primitive because they originate from a particular tribe or part of the country, that is why we call the Anglophones "*anglofou*" because we think they are stupid or Biafra because we consider them foreigners in their own country Cameroon, that is why names like *come-no-go* came into existence.

On another level, we blacks in America cry out loud when we are victims of discrimination. Then we turn around and discriminate against the Asians, Hispanics and other minorities and think it is okay. These other minority groups also behave in like manner, like the Chinese looking down on blacks, Hispanics, Indians and so on. Racism is not only a vice when committed by a majority race, it is deplorable when practiced by any human being, minority races included. What I am saying is that as we point fingers at other people, we need to also examine ourselves and be sure we are not showing double standards."

"That is some profound talk my friend; food for thought" Albert concluded.

Albert enjoyed the rest of his stay in America. Some friends pressured him to stay on but he would rather be content with what he had in Cameroon than chase an apparently elusive dream. Besides, the idea of concocting an asylum case was disturbing.

He agreed with Paul Davis; "If you don't feel it, flee from it. Go where you are celebrated, not merely tolerated."

When time came, Albert boarded his flight with a "Good bye America, Cameroon here I come back. The pasture may actually be greener here for some but it takes a tremendous amount of work and dedication to keep it that way" attitude.

With that, he joined the group nicknamed *when-I-was,* those that started and ended every conversation with "when I was in America." This was also their favorite pick up line. Nyamnjoh referred to these as *been-to* and amongst them also exists the concept of relative superiority. One says to the other "You stayed in America for only two weeks, you are not a real *been-to.* I am better than you because I was there for six months or more."

Note to the reader

I hope you enjoyed reading this book. My editor raised a few concerns after reading this book and I am guessing that many readers might have the same questions. Consequently I have preemptively addressed some of those questions.

Do I have some stereotypes about Cameroonians/Africans, the way they behave, react and interact? Am I a little mean?

It is not my intention to be mean. Frank talk can seem mean. I felt that way while reading *The Disillusioned African* by Francis Nyamnjoh but hard truth should be hard hitting. Before you complain too strongly about any stereotypes remember that I am a Cameroonian who also lives abroad and my strong rhetoric could in part be a message to the man in the mirror.

You might also be wondering why most people I profile in this book either live or have lived shady lives. Is it my intention to portray Cameroonians as opportunists, people not to be trusted, gold diggers, morally depraved, people who live in tensional relationships, etc.?

No, this is not a representation of all Cameroonians. I know many honest, faithful, trustworthy, hardworking Cameroonians who live in very good and healthy relationships. I also know some police officers, administrators and government officials that perform their duties with a high degree of honesty and respect. I had a story to tell and I profiled people that provided a platform for my story. What is good doesn't need fixing. The great Cameroonians at home and abroad shine bright and it was not my intention to profile them at this time. However, if you are concerned that a person with little knowledge about Cameroon will come to a general conclusion based on a few profiled individuals, I will tend to agree that it is not unfounded. A learned professor in the Queendom (to borrow from Nyamnjoh) once asked my friend and I how often we shaved. "Twice a week" we both replied, to which he said "interesting. I didn't know that African men shaved only twice a week." At that point, according to him, two African men were a statistically significant and full representation of all African men. Hopefully such a far reaching conclusion will not be the case here.

You might also be wondering if we should emulate Albert as he takes the bold step to return to Cameroon. You might be asking if there is anything wrong with staying abroad. There is nothing wrong with staying abroad.

Samson is an example in my story that is happy abroad, has brought other people who have built successful lives abroad and clearly says that he will do it all over again if the clock were turned back. Staying abroad for most Cameroonians is a choice and for most it is probably not an informed choice. There is no doubt that many people jump into this adventure with a lot of assumptions.